Part 1

Chapter 1: The Death of the Queen

A ray of late afternoon sunlight pierced through the window and shone on the golden hair of Queen Torina as she lay in bed. She was called the Queen of Sun by the people of Minear, for she was radiant, the most beautiful queen the kingdom had ever known, and because her hair looked as if it were made of sunlight itself. But now she was very ill, startlingly gaunt and a sickly pale. She was not long for the world, just as the setting sun outside the healing house was not long for the sky. She would be dead by the time it set. And indeed she already seemed dead, as did King Naelor who sat beside her. He looked upon her with an expression so grave and miserable that one who saw him would surely believe his heart was broken in two inside him. Yet his eyes were dry, and he sat completely still—so still that he appeared a statue, a great old statue sculpted in eternal grief, his thick head of black hair as dark as his spirit.

The door across the room opened slowly, and a tall, thin man entered gravely, his hands on the shoulders of a small boy. Each had hair like the king's, for they were his younger brother and son: Prince Nadir and Prince Taelor. The boy was six years of age, but seemed younger, for he was extraordinarily little; King Naelor wished his son were taller and stronger.

The young Prince Taelor's eyes were red as tears streamed from them. He felt guilty as he sobbed, for his father would always scorn him when he wept. But surely weeping would be permitted over such a cause.

At the sound of her son, Queen Torina returned to life. Her head rolled in his direction, and she said, weakly, "My sweet child."

Taelor's throat was too sore and tight to utter a greeting in response. Prince Nadir put a gentle hand to the boy's back and led him closer to his mother's bed. Queen Torina looked into the face of her son, her eyes full of love, and said, "Taelor, I would have thy sweet smile be the last thing I see. Would thou smile for me?"

But Taelor could not smile, for he could not understand why his mother would want him to be happy over her departure, never to return to hold him or care for him.

King Naelor sat utterly still. He made no acknowledgment of his son or brother, too caught up in his own despair.

Prince Nadir, eyes brimmed with tears, put his arms around Taelor's shoulders once again, and said, "Smile, Taelor. For thy mother. Please."

At this point, Taelor was agitated. Why were his mother and uncle telling him to smile? To young Taelor, this was not a time to be happy.

"Taelor," Queen Torina spoke, putting her hand to her child's face.

"I'm not smiling," he blurted suddenly, the tight feeling in his throat relieved at his annoyance. "How can I smile when you are going to sleep forever?"

Then he burst into tears once again and stormed out the door. Prince Nadir followed after him. Queen Torina died.

~

A week after his beloved wife's passing, King Naelor saw beyond his own grief and realized that Taelor, too, was hurting profoundly. When the boy was not crying, which was a rare find, he was moping around; no longer did he find joy in playing outside, practicing his swordsmanship or archery, or riding ponies. Naelor now not only felt pain from the untimely death of his wife, but also from his son's sorrow, so he bought Taelor his own horse, a foal that he could grow with and form a bond with from a young age.

The foal was ebony and brown with white legs and small white patches on its body, its mane and tail a jet black. Taelor fell in love with it and seldom left its side. He found it simultaneously elegant and masculine. It was a beautiful, regal horse, and young Taelor saw in it the same characteristics that he saw in Minear, his father's kingdom, his future kingdom.

Indeed, the horse seemed to him the kingdom of Minear in animal form, so he named it Minny.

King Naelor also noted that with his mother gone, Taelor would need a maternal figure to raise him, so he hired a kindly old woman by the name of Miss Hale. Taelor liked Miss Hale from the start, for she smiled a lot and was good at telling stories. But she would never be his mother. However, after a month of having her as his nanny, Taelor grew to love her. Likewise, Miss Hale adored Taelor, as did the entire kingdom—he was a very handsome child, having inherited his mother's great beauty, and was always polite and mild of manner.

Chapter 2: Taelor and the Forest Halflings

After eight-year-old Prince Taelor got himself dressed, Miss Hale looked out his chamber window and smiled, for the weather was fair. The great stone walls of the castle, usually a drab grey hue, looked a soft, cheerful yellow in the morning sunshine.

"My, the weather is indeed lovely today!" Miss Hale said, turning to Taelor. "Let us go outside and enjoy it, what think thee?"

"Yes, I would like that," answered Taelor

Miss Hale smiled her sweet smile, holding her hand out to the young prince.

Taelor grabbed his nanny's hand, and the two walked through the corridor and down the stairway, to the great castle door. They crossed over the courtyard, and many of the nobles and domestics waved at Taelor and bowed or curtseyed before him. Taelor smiled graciously at them all.

Miss Hale and Taelor crossed the bridge which rested upon the circular moat that surrounded the castle. Outside on the grounds, they sat on the sweet grass. Miss Hale had brought a blanket for them both to sit on, as well as a book to read. But Taelor was not interested in the book. Although it happened to be one of his favorite stories, he was too familiar with it, and all he wanted to do was play on the grass.

"Very well," said Miss Hale, "I will just read to myself, then."

But she could not help but watch Taelor roll around on the grass, laughing with the carefree joy that belonged solely to children. She wished she had half the energy and half the cheerfulness of this little boy.

Taelor stopped his rolling and sat up, grinning at his nanny. She walked over to him and looked at his grass-stained clothes, shaking her head. Then she began picking grass from his wavy black hair, which was now a complete mess.

"I know not why I bother making thee look so comely," she said with a sigh.

"Because I am the prince, King Naelor's only son, and the future king," responded the boy, a cheeky glint in his eye.

"Yes, that thou art!" Miss Hale chuckled. "Now, will thou sit here like a good little prince and let me read to thee?"

Reluctantly, Taelor joined his nanny on the blanket, and she read the tale of Sir Kayden the Bold. But Taelor, being familiar with this story, paid little attention; instead, he gazed around, wishing he was still playing on the grass. And the forest some hundred yards north grabbed his attention.

"Can't we go in there?" interrupted Taelor, pointing toward the thick of trees.

"The woods?" said Miss Hale. "Strange things happen in the woods, dear."

"Please," he whined, "Just for a bit."

Miss Hale sighed. "Well, thou art the prince and future king. If thou wish it, we will go."

Taelor jumped up and started heading in the direction of the forest.

"Get not too far ahead of me now!" Miss Hale called after him as he ran.

When Taelor arrived at the edge of the forest, he was panting. Miss Hale struggled behind, so he waited for his nanny to catch up. Terribly short of breath, Miss Hale leaned against a tree.

Taelor was filled with wonder at the forest. The trees were so tall, and the woods were so deep that he thought they went on forever. He felt as if he had entered a different world.

"Not too far now," called Miss Hale, wheezing, pointing a strict finger at Taelor.

But Taelor had heard a couple of funny, high-pitched voices just slightly deeper within the woods, and he became curious. He looked around eagerly, trying to spot whoever had spoken, but could not see anyone. He walked on a bit further.

"Little prince," Miss Hale cried, "Stop thy wandering!"

But Taelor, his mind concentrated on finding the beings that these strange voices belonged to, did not hear his nanny. And he was now far out of her sight. But Miss Hale, being too exhausted to move, could only call out after him, yelling, "Taelor! Taelor! Come back!"

Just to his left, Taelor caught sight of something moving, but it disappeared in a flash. Afraid, he let out a yelp and ran behind a nearby tree.

Then the beings that Taelor had sought after became aware of his presence, and like him, grew curious.

They popped out suddenly, and Taelor, peeking from behind the tree, could see them clearly. Looking upon their faces, he was no longer afraid, for they looked friendly. Indeed, they were just little people. They were even shorter than Taelor himself, a small child of eight, yet their faces were those of fully-grown women—rather old women, in fact. Taelor was baffled.

He stepped out and approached them. The little women stared at him in awe, seeming just as bewildered about him as he was about them.

"That is a very tall boy... He's one of the Big Folk. I've never seen one up close," said one of the little women to the other, but loud enough so Taelor could hear.

Confused, Taelor replied, "I'm actually rather small for my age."

The little women gasped. "We speak the same tongue," said one, her eyes wide.

The other then nudged her and said, "We are being impolite. Let us introduce ourselves to the boy, then."

Noticing Taelor's royal garb, the funny women curtseyed before him in a most clumsy fashion, and in unison said, "We call ourselves the Glade Litterer and the Stalk Squeaker. We are Forest Halflings," and each pointed to herself when she spoke her name.

Taelor found these Forest Halflings, as they called themselves, most peculiar, and they amused him. But he showed no signs of amusement in his face, for he was a polite young man. He smiled and said, "'Tis a pleasure to meet you both. I am Prince Taelor."

The Forest Halflings gasped once again and clapped their hands to their mouths.

"*The* Prince, in *our* woods?"

Taelor grinned proudly and nodded his head.

The two Forest Halflings stared at him in bewilderment. Then the Glade Litterer, coming to her senses, realized that it was rude to stare. She nudged the Stalk Squeaker, and the two composed their facial expressions.

"Shall we invite him over for cake and tea?" the Glade Litterer asked of the Stalk Squeaker.

And the Stalk Squeaker asked, "Do princes like cake and tea?"

"Everyone likes cake and tea," said the Glade Litterer. "And he is a child. What child does not like cake?"

Taelor thought it strange that they were discussing him like this when he was right there in their presence. He concluded that these Forest Halflings must not have much interaction with other people.

"I do like cake and tea," Taelor spoke up.

At this, the two Forest Halflings jumped and squealed.

"Superb," the Glade Litterer sang. "Do come in, we'd love to have you."

Then the Stalk Squeaker suddenly looked uneasy. "We should not just invite a child into our home, especially the prince! What would his parents think of that? The *king* and *queen*? Our home is not fit for royalty! No, no, not at all, not in the slightest."

Taelor felt sad. He had taken quite a liking to the Forest Halflings, and he fancied cake and tea now that they had been offered. But what made him saddest of all was the mention of the queen, for his mother had died of a mortal illness just two years past. He looked down at the ground, and his eyes welled with tears, one of which came trickling down his cheek.

The Glade Litterer slapped the Stalk Squeaker on the arm. "Oh, look what you've done!" she snapped, "You've made him cry."

The Stalk Squeaker looked immensely guilty, and the two Forest Halflings approached Taelor from either side, repeatedly patting his shoulder, thinking this might comfort him. Taelor thought these Forest Halflings weirder by the minute.

"I'm okay," he said, wishing for them to stop.

"I meant not to upset you, Prince Taelor," said the Stalk Squeaker earnestly, her eyes looking upon him with pity.

Taelor now felt bad. "Mind not," he said, "You knew not that my mother is dead."

"Oh no!" the Forest Halflings cried, and they flung their arms around him.

"I'm so sorry," said the Stalk Squeaker.

"He is certainly in need of cake and tea now!" exclaimed the Glade Litterer.

"Yes, indeed," agreed the Stalk Squeaker.

They both took him by the hand and led him through the forest, guiding him to their home. After twisting and turning between many a tree, the Forest Halflings finally halted. Taelor wondered why, for there was just an open patch of ground here, no home to be seen.

Then the Forest Halflings knelt and moved aside various twigs and leaves, revealing an opening, a tunnel leading underground.

"Here it is," said the Glade Litterer, and she slid down it. Then Taelor and the Stalk Squeaker heard her voice call out, "Come down, Prince Taelor, and make yourself at home!"

But Taelor was hesitant. "Just how far down is it?" he asked the Stalk Squeaker warily.

And she replied, "Oh, not far down at all, really. You'll reach the bottom before you know it."

Then Taelor sat at the mouth of the tunnel, but he was afraid.

"Shall I give you a nudge?" the Stalk Squeaker suggested.

But before Taelor could respond, she had pushed him, and he went sliding down. The surface was smooth and muddy, and he went with speed, screaming all the way. But as the Stalk Squeaker had said, he reached the bottom before long, and he was in the home of the Forest Halflings. He looked about him, mouth agape and eyes wide. It was the coziest place he had ever seen; small and modest, but with all the comforts of home. The place was dimly lit yet cheerful, and there were two armchairs with cushions by a fireplace, a wooden table to dine at, and a shelf filled with a collection of delicate teapots and teacups.

The Stalk Squeaker slid down shortly after, and she looked at Taelor. "Well, what think you of our humble abode, young prince?" she asked.

Taelor, still gazing around, said, "I love it!"

The Glade Litterer chuckled and looked upon him fondly. "You are indeed very polite," she said, then in a humble tone, "But I doubt you do. After all, what is this compared to a castle?"

"I *do* love it, really," said Taelor, "I've never seen a home like this."

The two Forest Halflings were flattered by his sincere adoration of their home. Then the Stalk Squeaker retrieved a bucket of water that she had earlier gotten from the River Ceden, east of the forest, and started a fire to heat it for their tea. The Glade Litterer brought out a big plate veiled with yellow cloth and set it on the wooden table in the corner of the room. Then she sat at the table and bid Taelor join her.

"So tell me, Prince Taelor, are there any other princes in Minear, or princesses?" she asked.

"There is one other prince," said Taelor, "My uncle, Prince Nadir. But no princesses."

"No princesses?" exclaimed the Glade Litterer, "And how old is your uncle?"

"I know not his age," said Taelor, "But he's my father's younger brother."

"Why does he not have a wife?" asked the Glade Litterer.

"I'm not sure," said Taelor, and he had never thought it strange until that moment.

Then the Stalk Squeaker intervened with, "Why, thou art nosy, Glade Litterer. Harass not our guest with such questions."

So instead, the Glade Litterer asked Taelor if he knew any good stories to tell, and excitedly he told some of his favorite tales: Sir Kayden the Bold, The Tale of the Ruby Locket, and The Lady of the Sapphire Cave. Both the Forest Halflings listened with eager ears, and soon, the tea was prepared, and they removed the yellow cloth from the plate, revealing a hearty pound cake.

"I made it fresh this morning," said the Glade Litterer.

"It smells delicious," said Taelor, "What's in it?"

"You best not ask, young prince," said the Stalk Squeaker, "Glade Litterer over here gets a bit carried away when she bakes. She throws in whatever her hands touch."

At this, Taelor's facial expression became alarmed.

"Oh, listen not to her!" said the Glade Litterer. "My cakes are superb. In this one, I put in leaves, flowers, and various berries."

Taelor looked uneasy. "Are you sure the berries… aren't poisonous?"

The Glade Litterer laughed, "Of course I am! Here, I'll taste a spoonful first; then you can eat it."

And so she did, and Taelor, seeing that the Glade Litterer had no negative reaction to the cake, dug in his spoon and tried some. He was pleasantly surprised at how tasty the cake was, and then he took a much bigger second spoonful. The tea was delightful, also, and the Forest Halflings were showing him excellent hospitality. Plus, they liked his stories so much that they asked him to tell more. So Taelor enthusiastically told them all that he knew of the classic tales of legend.

Meanwhile, time went by, and back in the castle of Minear, the king's mind was troubled and his heart anxious. Miss Hale, having searched the woods for Taelor for some hours, finally had to turn away and make her way back. When she told King Naelor that she had lost his son in the woods, he grew red in the face and sentenced her to death. So Miss Hale now sat in a cold, hard prison cell, awaiting her hanging at the morn.

King Naelor sent out a search party of seven knights to find Taelor. And although those who were chosen felt honored, and of course were whole-heartedly willing to rescue their future king, they were nervous, for superstition called these woods the "Dark Forest" and strange tales had come from there.

~

Back in the home of the Forest Halflings, Taelor suddenly became aware of how long he had spent with the Glade Litterer and Stalk Squeaker and became worried.

"I must find my nanny!" he blurted suddenly. "I wandered off and left her. She must be looking for me."

"Oh dear!" cried the Forest Halflings, and they got up from their seats. "We'll help you find her, Big Little Prince, don't you worry."

They climbed up the same tunnel from which they had entered, pulling themselves along with the rope of vines attached to the wall. Once they were again out within the circle of trees, the Forest Halflings hastily concealed the entrance to their home, then led Taelor back to where they had met him, at the southern edge of the forest. They looked around them as they went, calling for Miss Hale, but there was no sign of her. Then suddenly, out ahead, glimmers of blue were seen passing amongst the trees. The Forest Halflings were afraid, and they stood back. But Taelor moved in closer to get a better look. These were Minear knights, their capes of blue flowing from behind their shining armor.

"You need not fear," Taelor called out to the Glade Litterer and Stalk Squeaker, "These are my father's knights. They must have come to retrieve me."

But as he turned to look back at them, the Forest Halflings were nowhere to be seen. He hurried over to where they were just moments before and gazed around, but they were out of sight. He felt a sudden loneliness and sense of betrayal, for he thought these Forest Halflings were his friends… yet now they had deserted him, scurrying away out of fright, without a parting word.

Taelor ran over to the knights, calling, "Here I am, knights! Here I am!"

A few turned their heads, and as they saw him running toward them, joyous smiles spread across their faces. "The prince is found!" they called, "Let us bring him home!"

So glad were they to see that Taelor was safe and unharmed. And Sir Hebnor, who loved Taelor like his own, picked him up and set him on his shoulders, bearing him back to the castle. Taelor told the knights of the Forest Halflings, and although the knights showed interest in all he had to say of them, they dismissed his tale as the wild imaginings of a child.

Taelor was brought to the throne room and returned to his father. King Naelor sat on the black marble throne, a large black marble hawk with outspread wings towering high from the back of the rest, deep blue drapes of silk hanging from its talons and touching the floor. As the king spotted young Taelor, so relieved was he that he laughed out of sheer joy, the first time he had laughed since his wife was taken from him. He stepped down from the throne and rushed over to Taelor, got down on his knees, and embraced him. Taelor could not recall ever being held by his father like this.

"I was so worried! I love thee, Taelor," the king spoke into his son's shoulder. "Thou must not go wandering off again. I thought I had lost thee!"

Then the king released his son, and looked upon him, a smile still brightening his face. "But here thou art, safe and sound. My dear boy…"

Taelor felt guilty. "I love you, too, Father," he said, "And I will not wander off again. I should not have left Miss Hale, my poor old nanny. Where is she?"

At this, the king's face returned to its typical stern expression, and he rose to his feet.

"She is in a prison cell, and will be hanged at dawn," he said, "Losing the future king in the Dark Forest is, of course, a crime punishable by death."

Taelor felt crushed to the ground by this news.

"No!" he cried, "Please show mercy, Father! It was my fault! I went off, and she was too out of breath to follow after me!"

But even his son's distress could not sway Naelor's mind.

"Thou art too forgiving, Taelor," he spoke, "She was thy nanny. Her one job was to look after thee. She failed at her job, and the consequences could have been grave if luck—or destiny—had not kept thee safe. Thou could have been hurt, Taelor. Or killed—leaving Minear without its rightful heir, and me with a broken heart."

Taelor's eyes filled with tears, and he turned away and left the throne room with his head hung low. A guard escorted him to his chamber, and Taelor climbed into bed and wept into his pillow.

Prince Nadir, who was present in the throne room, turned to the king and said, "Will you not show mercy, for the sake of your son? He has already lost his mother. Let him not lose his nanny now."

Naelor looked at his younger brother, his face hard, and in a venomous tone, said, "Dost thou speak out against thy king?"

"No, Your Grace," said Nadir, "I speak only as an uncle who cares for his nephew."

At this, King Naelor was riled. "Dost thou imply that thou care for him more than I?"

"Nay, Your Grace. Never," said Nadir. "I think only that the boy has been through enough, and that you need not add more grief to his childhood."

"So thou resent my judgment? Fine. I care not," said the king. "Thou hast always been too soft for thy own good... I will not have my son turn out the same. In fact, he will be there at Miss Hale's execution tomorrow, standing by my side. That will make the lesson sink in."

Nadir shook his head in disagreement. "That is cruel."

"Life is cruel, little brother."

Nadir gave up. "So be it," he said. "Yet my heart forebodes that if you are to continue harming those who Taelor loves, he will turn on you."

Naelor felt a cold shadow creep upon him, but coolly he said, "Nonsense. A son respects his father."

"Yes," said Nadir, "But respect can be lost."

And with that, Prince Nadir turned and exited the throne room, and King Naelor was left uneasy.

~

The next day came with fine weather once again, but Taelor rebuked it. He felt that it mocked him. He wondered why such an evil day could have sunshine and blue sky.

A manservant had awoken him, and in his mood, Taelor sent him away after his breakfast was brought, saying that he could dress himself and that he had no further need for him.

At the execution, Taelor stood at King Naelor's side. Miss Hale was ungently brought up onto the platform, and as the noose was placed around her neck, Taelor looked away. But upon noticing this, Naelor looked down at Taelor and bid him watch. So Taelor obeyed his father and looked on as the surface on which Miss Hale stood was dropped, her body falling limp at the snap of her neck.

Taelor's chest felt hollow and his eyes stung, but he put all his strength behind not weeping. Then as Naelor looked down at Taelor and saw that no tears filled his eyes, he felt proud. He placed a hand on his son's shoulder and gave him a firm nod.

So passed the second traumatic event of Taelor's life, of which there were many to come. His childhood was lonely, and he was often a recluse in his chamber, reading all the books he could get his hands on, having a strong desire for knowledge and a passion for tales of legend. His visit with the Forest Halflings had cost him much but lit a fire for knowledge of what mystical things lay outside Minear.

When he approached manhood, he grew tall, and his strength was greater than what his slender stature promised. He was a fine swordsman, too, and quick and agile in combat. But he did not have a love for weaponry or battle like his father.

Chapter 3: The Tea Witch's Cloak

Prince Taelor was sitting at his desk, alone in his chamber. It was the seventeenth year of his life and the eleventh anniversary of his mother's passing. On such a date, his mood was melancholic. He was reading through a history book that was laid flat on the oak table, the long and slender fingers of his right hand around a chalice of wine, when his father, King Naelor, knocked on his chamber door. Taelor permitted him entry.

Approaching his son, the king laid a gentle hand on his shoulder and said, "I am often so caught up in my own mourning on this date that I forget to see how thou art doing. Might I join thee?"

Taelor gestured to the seat beside him, and said, "I always have an empty sort of feeling on this date. I wish I had a better memory of Mother."

"Thy mother was my everything," the king replied, his voice thick with grief. "Thou art so like her. Thou hast her gentle heart and calm demeanor. And thou prefer to sit inside and read, very unlike how I was at thy age." The king gave a small smile. "Yes, thou art indeed like thy mother; in face, also, but thou hast my hair."

Taelor felt the tears come to his eyes, so he stared down blankly at his history book. He sat quietly for a while, but then said, "I have often felt like you were disappointed in me, that you resented how I prefer to read than practice my swordsmanship, archery, or knife throwing…"

The king's expression softened as he said, "Disappointed? No. You are my one and only, and I wouldn't trade you for another. You are a good swordsman, but yes, I have often wished you were as eager to be a great warrior as I was in my youth. However, never disappointed. Besides, I was the middle child of three sons growing up; therefore, my life was never as valuable as yours. You are my heir, my only heir, so perhaps 'tis a good thing you prefer to sit and read and have a thirst for knowledge rather than glory."

Taelor smiled. "Would you have had more children, if Mother had not died?"

"I am not sure," answered the king.

"I suppose that if I were born a daughter, however, you would have tried for another before I could walk," said Taelor.

"Well, yes, for the Pevrel name. I would have a Pevrel sit on the throne of Minear for many generations to come, if not forever. My older brother, Naygur, died before he could have a legitimate child, though I'm sure he fathered many bastards. And Nadir's liking for pretty young men and his stubbornness, or selfishness, prevented him from ever marrying and putting a son in a woman."

Taelor met eyes with his father. "I like it not when you talk about Uncle like that," he said.

Naelor gave something of a shrug. "I suppose that on this date we should be remembering thy Mother and not how Nadir has disgraced our House. Or how Naygur did, for that matter." He let out a sorrowful sigh. "House Pevrel was so great once… Our ancestors possessed the gift of foresight and used it for battle strategy, winning kingdoms left and right. Pevrel was the most powerful and respected House on the continent. Our words, 'A Hawk's Eyes See All' used to send a shiver down the spine of every man from a lesser House. And now what? They are but a vestige of our glory from the ancient days, and that is all."

Taelor had his eyes fixed on a corner of the room. He was thinking back on all the fantastical accounts he had read of House Pevrel in his history books. Rather than being bitter about House Pevrel having lost their former glory, Taelor was proud to have the blood of those greats running through his veins. He didn't care if House Pevrel was not what is once was. History remained, and the books would tell many generations yet to come.

But finally, Naelor said, "*You* must be great, Taelor."

Taelor hated it when his father talked like that. He didn't need even more pressure laid on him.

"I will do what I can, Father," he said, somewhat dismissively. He did not bother asking what his father would have him do, because he knew that Naelor had no straight answer. He was just proud and ever hungry for glory.

"Duty," said Naelor with a nod. "And 'tis not a half-bad thing when it means getting a beautiful wife, is it? In a fortnight thou wilt marry the lovely Lady Ethellas from Haseidin."

"I am happy," said Taelor.

"May thy happiness with her last longer than mine," said Naelor with concealed bitterness in his voice. "I would a thousand of my men die and your mother still live."

"I know," said Taelor tenderly. "I the same. But a thousand men should not die."

"Forget them," Naelor snapped. "Your mother was worth a thousand men and more. She was everything."

For the first time, the king let his stone-cold front dissolve in front of his son, allowing himself to weep. Taelor could not recognize this weeping man as his father. Still, in his awe, he placed a comforting hand on the king's shoulder. Naelor, with a start, dried his eyes and got to his feet.

"On the morrow, my son," he said, barely looking at Taelor, and retired from Taelor's chambers.

~

Deep in the forest, where the trees were tall and many, there was a dingy old cottage smothered with overgrown, blackened plants. In this cottage there lived a peculiar old woman with a long chin and grey complexion, her hair scraggly and white, and her tatty cloak a dark brown. She called herself the Tea Witch. Oftentimes, she was visited by her merry (though also peculiar) dumpy friends, the Glade Litterer and the Stalk Squeaker, who would always be more than ready to run little errands for the Tea Witch, usually with silly smiles on their good-natured faces.

On one occasion when these two were over, the three odd women were sitting at the table enjoying carrot cake. The Tea Witch got up and entered into her cluttered little kitchen and made to prepare tea. But for some reason, she was having great difficulty starting a fire, and so called upon the Glade Litterer and Stalk Squeaker to do it.

But the Stalk Squeaker said, "Is there really a need for fire? If you're a witch, surely you can boil water using your powers?"

To this comment, the Tea Witch lifted up the tail of her tattered brown cloak and whacked the Stalk Squeaker over the head with it.

"Ouch, what was that for?" the Stalk Squeaker cried.

"For being a cheeky little imp, that's what! Now get to work, the both of thee!"

The Stalk Squeaker apologized, but corrected the Tea Witch, explaining that neither she nor the Glade Litterer was an imp. To this, the Tea Witch said that she was merely using figurative language and that her two friends would do well not to question her abilities, nor be over-sensitive when she called them names.

Now after a while, the two dumpy ones had gotten a little fire going, and they heated up the pan of water.

"Superb!" exclaimed the Tea Witch, "And as we are about to prepare tea, I see it fit to speak to thee both of my latest plan. In the near future, I shall make some special tea which I will send to that young prince down the way; and when he drinks it, my enchantment upon it shall make him walk and talk funny for a whole week!"

The Glade Litterer then looked up at the Tea Witch and said, "But why ever would you do that? Prince Taelor is ever so handsome, and it would be such a shame for him to come across so uncouth."

The Tea Witch sighed. "Have thee no sense of humor whatsoever?" she snapped, making the dumpy ones jump. "If this comes to be—which it shall—it will be the most amusing calamity of the whole decade!"

And indeed a few days later, the Tea Witch made a teapot full of tea and laid her enchantment upon it. She then made her way to the castle of Minear and using her powers, disguised herself as a young maid. She entered the castle's halls and passed the teapot on to a real maid, saying that it was under the prince's command and that he desired it immediately. The maid, having no reason to suspect the Tea Witch or her word, hastened to the prince's personal servant, Leygon, a young chap with a bright face and curly blond hair, and told him to deliver the tea to his master. So he did. The prince, confused yet content, drank it by the fire. Immediately the effects showed on him: when he stood, he had a hunchback, and his arms hung down limp at his sides. His knees became bent, and when he spoke, his voice sounded screechy and very silly. In a panic, he went as quickly as he could to the king's halls, seeking his father. In great distress did the king look upon his son, for he did not know what had come over him so suddenly, nor what could have caused such symptoms.

On top of everything, it was most unfortunate timing. It was arranged for Prince Taelor to wed the Lady Ethellas of the kingdom of Haseidin, who would be arriving the following day. Haseidin was the westernmost country of the eastern continent and Ethellas and her family, with their domestics, had sailed the Wide Sea and arrived at the shore of Tyniad. They had been traveling in their carriage from Tyniad for two full days now.

"It was the tea!" cried Taelor in his strange new voice.

When the king noticed that there was even something wrong with his son's speech, he went into a great panic.

King Naelor summoned two of his messengers and five of his knights. To the messengers, he gave the errand of tracking down the Lady Ethellas and her family on their travels to give tidings that Prince Taelor was very unwell and that the marriage was to be postponed. To the knights, he gave the errand of finding and killing the person or creature responsible for the hideous spell that was laid upon his son.

"I imagine the being who did this to Prince Taelor to have come from the Dark Forest down yonder," spoke the king, "Strange are the legends of that place, and whenever queer incidents like this occur, always they seem to lead thither. There are none in Minear who know what inhabitants dwell amongst those tall trees, but whoever, or whatever, dwells within must surely be evil. Be wary, for none can foretell what perils may await you within the forest. You shall depart at dawn."

The two messengers, however, were equipped with horses and sent out immediately. But they could not find the carriage, no matter how many routes they tried. They decided in dismay that they must have missed it and that it would arrive at Minear before they could prevent it.

Inside her carriage, the Lady Ethellas spoke excitedly of meeting Prince Taelor. Wonderful things she had heard of him; that he was gallant and noble-hearted, and the most handsome of all the men in the kingdom, with wavy, dark shoulder-length hair, pale skin, and "eyes like two full moons" as they would say. And likewise, Taelor had heard wonderful things of Ethellas: that she was elegant and charming and very beautiful, with a dark brown complexion, shiny black hair, and sparkly eyes. So indeed, why would two young hearts oppose?

~

The next day as the sun rose, the Tea Witch awoke with a conniving smile on her wrinkly face. She was excited because she had been planning to go into Minear's castle again, for a second time disguising herself as a maid, to see if she could spy on the prince and laugh at what her tea had done to him. To save her little friends from idleness, she set errands for them. To the Stalk Squeaker she gave the chore of dusting her cottage, and to the Glade Litterer she gave the task of searching for herbs, presenting her with a list of specific herbs that she wanted. As was their custom, the pair of half-sized women smiled and nodded and immediately made themselves busy. The Tea Witch set out and began her long walk through the forest and to the kingdom of Minear.

Also, in the early hours of the day, the five knights appointed by the king set out on their quest. Each man had a heavy heart, wondering if he was to return. Once they had entered the forest, after about an hour and a half of searching under the shadows of the ominous trees, finally they found the creature they assumed was behind the spell: a short, squat, funny-looking person who seemed to be acting most suspiciously, ruffling through the grass and the plants. Since this was the only person they had seen in the forest, and because they wanted to get out of that loathsome place as quickly as possible, they immediately decided this must be the one the king wanted them to kill. A few of the men set arrows to their bows and made ready to shoot. They waited upon the command of Sir Paldir, and when finally he said "shoot," their arrows sang through the air, and their target fell dead. The men then rode toward the body and picked it up and took it back to Minear with them, as proof they had completed their task.

Once the knights had gotten back to the castle, they went to the king and showed him the body. The king smiled upon them and congratulated them. He then went off in search of his son to see if the enchantment was lifted. But lo! The king found Prince Taelor in his chamber, and both his posture and voice were unchanged.

Still, King Naelor explained to his son what befell in the forest; that all of the five knights were returned and that they had killed a creature who they had suspected of placing the cruel enchantment upon him. Then, wishing not to speak in his silly voice, Taelor got up and grabbed a piece of parchment, a quill, and ink. He went to his wooden desk in the middle of his chamber and wrote in his steady, elegant hand, "What kind of creature was it that the knights slew?"

And after the king gave his description, Taelor sighed, and with a pained countenance, he wrote: "That was one of the Forest Halflings. They are a peaceful people and do not practice enchantments, so it could not have been one of them who did this to me. This I know, for I have read much lore on them. My heart grieves that an innocent life should be taken on my behalf."

After reading what Taelor had written, the king put his hand on his son's shoulder and said, "My boy, carry not the weight of a dead 'Halfling.'"

And with that, King Naelor left.

~

Whilst the knights were still in the forest, the Tea Witch arrived in sight of the castle and began to place the disguise enchantment upon herself. However, she was spotted by the court blacksmith before she could complete the disguise.

"Hey!" he shouted at her, "Hey you! Who are you, and what are you doing here?"

Startled and frightened, the Tea Witch ran around a corner, and to her good luck, came across a forgotten laundry basket. Deciding to quickly change her clothing rather than disguise herself as a young maid, as the spell took a while and she needed haste, she threw off her tattered brown cloak, carelessly leaving it on the ground, and rummaged through the clothing in the laundry basket. When she found a pale-yellow dress that looked her size, she slipped it on and ran away at a speed not expected of someone her age. The blacksmith had not seen where she went off to, and she managed to escape quite smoothly. But still, the blacksmith told of his suspicious sighting to a couple of knights, and once they informed the king, Naelor set up a strict watch guard, and ordered them to kill this dodgy character if they were to spot her.

In the late afternoon, the Lady Ethellas arrived in Minear with her brother, mother, and stepfather, King Raylir. The guards saw the carriage arriving in its splendor and spotted the orange flag with the hyena of House Polat. Some winded their horns, and others rode to King Naelor. In dismay, Naelor fetched his son.

"But... but... I thought the marriage had been postponed!" Taelor cried in his ridiculous voice. "I can't possibly wed the Lady Ethellas like this!"

"They obviously did not receive the tidings, I am afraid, my son. But as they are here, thou hast no choice. And who can tell? Perhaps the condition will be gone by morning! The morrow at ten o'clock is when the union of the Houses Pevrel and Polat is to be. Rest well this night, and perhaps it will pass."

And so it was that Ethellas met Taelor whilst the prince was under the enchantment of the tea, and expecting a man of grace and charm, she found herself quite disappointed. Taelor might have been very handsome, but he was repulsive with his disgraceful posture and pathetic-sounding voice. Lady Ethellas, however, was even more beautiful and graceful than Taelor had imagined, and he cursed his cruel affliction now more than ever.

Not long after the two betrothed first met, King Raylir of Haseidin called upon his servants to bring over two small, clear glasses that had a layer of almost an inch of sand from the Heseidin desert resting inside. The betrothed stood side by side, watching as two Heseidi servants balanced a golden tray between them and as more servants placed the glasses on it and poured water from an ornate jug over the sand in each glass. King Raylir himself then added a tonic to the mix and stirred it vigorously with a small golden stick. He then reached into his purse and pulled forth a thin, sharp, two-sided needle. Taelor found himself feeling lightheaded, but he fought against it. Raylir asked for his forefinger, placed it atop the drink before Ethellas, and pricked it. Taelor winced silently as droplets of his blood fell into the liquid, crimson sinking down into the sand. Raylir then flipped the needle and did the same to Ethellas, over Taelor's drink.

"Now," said King Raylir in his thick Heseidi accent, "you will drink from your glasses, all the liquid at once. The tonic will make your heads light and happy and help you overcome your nerves and awkwardness upon meeting. You will consume each other's blood, so the liquid that gives each of you life is now inside the other, a part of the other. And you will swallow sand, as much as you can, so, Ethellas, you will know you come from the desert, and the desert will always be in you, and Prince Taelor, so you know you now have the desert in you, upon marrying my step-daughter." He clapped his hands together lightly, then raising his hands elegantly, he spoke, "Now drink."

Taelor and Ethellas drained their glasses as quickly as they could, each leaving behind a stubborn layer of sand which stuck to the glasses' bottoms. Raylir smiled between the two. "They will have many very beautiful children, I am sure," he said to King Naelor.

"Very beautiful children, no doubt," Naelor smiled back.

Lady Ethellas looked unpleased.

King Naelor had arranged a banquet for that night, in warm welcome of the Polats and in celebration of the union between Hawk and Hyena. Ethellas continued to look unpleased all throughout, eating and drinking in silence and not caring even to grant Taelor her glance. He felt heartbroken when she got up and stormed away after the main course. King Raylir followed her out, his face stern.

"What in the world, young lady?" he spoke softly but violently.

"I am sorry, step-father, but I just cannot wed Prince Taelor."

"This is not a matter of thy desire; do thou realize how mighty House Polat would be if we united with House Pevrel? Besides, why should thou wish not to wed the young prince? He is very pleasing to the eye, is he not?"

"Indeed, he is as fair of face as the rumors say; but where are the rumors, I ask, of his repulsive voice and appalling posture?"

"As King Naelor already explained to us, he is *enchanted*."

"Enchanted? As if sorcery and enchantments exist! Do you think me a fool?"

"Listen, Ethellas; I will hear no more of this." King Raylir's voice lost all hint of kindness. "Thou art to wed Prince Taelor on the morrow, willing or unwilling."

Defeated, the Lady Ethellas, with an indignant yet proud expression, followed her king back to the banquet, taking her seat next to Prince Taelor. The rest of the banquet was very awkward, and Leygon, Taelor's servant, had to refill the prince's chalice quite a few times.

The feast soon came to a close, and the guests started filing out, Lady Ethellas being the most eager to leave. Taelor, however, remained seated, staring down at the table before him. King Naelor eventually gave him a gentle nudge and told him to follow him out of the dining hall, but still, Taelor would not budge. With a sigh, Naelor pulled out Taelor's chair so that his arms could no longer reach the table they were resting on.

Taelor groaned and reluctantly arose, but with a purposeful wave of his arm, he knocked over the chalice in front of him. Then he also knocked over the plate he had eaten from, then the plate that Lady Ethellas had eaten from.

Shocked at his son's outburst, and exceedingly embarrassed, Naelor snapped, "Stop this!"

But Taelor continued to knock things from the table, at which Naelor grabbed his arms and pinned them behind his back.

"Thou art making a fool of thyself and hurting the Pevrel reputation," Naelor sharply whispered into his son's ear.

As he spoke, he gave Taelor's arms a yank, and a sharp pain spread throughout Taelor's left bicep. Naelor had used too much force and sprained it. Immediately the king felt guilty, aware that he was rougher than he intended. His grip loosened, and Taelor, whose anger had been ignited, took this opportunity to break free. With a swift motion, he tore away from his father's grip, spun around so that he was facing him, then made to throw a punch at the king's face. But Naelor, whose reflexes were sharp and whose arms were strong, grabbed Taelor's wrist and stilled the blow.

Naelor's face was hard, and he looked at Taelor with stern eyes full of surprise and disappointment. "How dare thee attempt to strike thy father and thy king," he said in a strained but severe tone.

Taelor himself looked shocked at his own actions. "I am sorry, Father, I know not what has come over me."

Naelor gave him a nod. "It is forgiven, my son," he said. "I know thou must be frustrated with this enchantment over thee, especially at such an occasion as this."

Taelor nodded his head, his eyes filling with tears that he quickly blinked away.

"Did I hurt thee just before?" Naelor asked with concern.

Taelor made no answer. "Come now," said Naelor, and he led Taelor out of the dining hall.

Taelor walked back up to his chamber and sat at his desk. He had made a fool of himself; had acted most brutish. He was appalled by his manner. *But was it really his fault?* In his temper he had savagely knocked over plates and cups from the table, but for good reason—here was a beautiful girl with whom he was arranged to marry, but she was repulsed by him in his present state. And as for the attempted strike at his father—none can say that it was unprovoked— the king had first hurt *him*. These things Taelor told himself, and again he felt a fire surge within him. He wondered why all this was happening to him, making him look so foolish and behave so uncouthly.

Now, more than ever, he desired a good one-on-one combat with the knights, as they did during training. Unable, however, to release his anger that way, he picked up the ornate glass bowl on his shelf and threw it across the room, where it collided with the far wall and shattered. Realizing what he had done, Taelor sat at his desk and put his head in his hands. That bowl had been dear to his mother, and it was one of the few tokens he still possessed of her.

He had only vague memories of his mother. But the memory of their last moment together, just before she died, was as clear in his mind as if it had happened but a fortnight past: his mother had told him to smile, wishing for his smiling face to be the last thing she would see. But Taelor did not smile. Instead, he ran out of the room, leaving his mother to die without her final wish being granted. Maybe it was he who killed her, for not smiling. He wondered if he was the reason for his mother's death. He let himself cry his guilt away, then slipped into bed, falling into a deep sleep.

The next day came, and Taelor awoke to the sound of birds singing outside his window at around seven o'clock. He would have dozed back off to sleep but for the jolt he felt as he remembered that he was to wed the Lady Ethellas this day. With woe, he felt still the effects of the enchantment, no less potent than they had been the past couple of days. He got himself out of bed and called for Leygon to bring him hot chocolate and breakfast. Sensing his master's distress, Leygon tried to lighten the mood, and upon leaving, gave him an encouraging pat on the back. Once Taelor had finished breakfast, with a sigh, he got himself dressed for the occasion, and Leygon placed a silver crown upon his brow. Tidings soon came to the prince, however, that the marriage was not to take place after all.

Wishing not to spend the rest of her life with a man who had such an off-putting voice and posture, and seeing no way out of the marriage, the Lady Ethellas decided to flee from Minear. At daybreak, she crept out of the castle. Because she was a Lady and a guest of honor, the guards did not question her or prevent her from leaving. As she stepped outside into the cool breeze of dawn and breathed the fresh air, it struck her that never before had she felt so free and independent.

She crept around the corner and wandered off a little, wondering which direction she should take. When she came across a tattered brown cloak on the ground, it seemed like a sign to her that she ought to conceal her identity. She picked it up, slipped it over her head, and made sure also to put on the hood. Then she headed to the stables, took a horse, and rode off, her heart singing in victory. However, the finding of the Tea Witch's cloak proved her doom, for the watch guard spotted her and observed that she fit the Witch's description. Since Lady Ethellas's clandestine departure was unknown to them, they took her for the Witch and shot arrows at her. The Lady Ethellas fell dead.

When they saw the body and looked upon the face of the one they had slain, the knights felt such regret and fear that some took their own lives right then and there, to escape a worse fate. Others, however, felt it was their duty to own up to their evil mistake and face their awaiting doom with honor. Calling upon King Naelor, and the king and queen of Haseidin, they revealed to them the body of the Lady Ethellas. Queen Ethil sobbed hysterically once her initial shock had passed, and King Raylir stood as one turned to stone, tears falling from his eyes. King Naelor turned very pale, and no words were able to escape his lips. Once the news had reached the ears of Prince Taelor, so great was his grief that the enchantment of the tea broke, and he was himself again, save for the pang he felt in his chest.

Part 2

Chapter 4: The Bastard Princess

The sun shone brightly, and the birds sang sweetly that morning in Tyniad, a neighboring kingdom to Minear. Lady Alene looked out the window longingly, gazing up and down the courtyard. Her mother lay in bed, sleeping for now, though Alene knew that she would awake soon enough. When she did, Alene would have to see to her needs and make sure she ate and drank. Lady Elanna had been sick for weeks, and Alene hadn't left her side. Alene had on a simple gown, her long black hair tied in a bun. She waited upon her sick mother with tired eyes. Still staring out the window, now lost in a daydream, she was brought back to consciousness at the sound of her mother's groan. She rushed over to her bedside.

"My dear Alene, look not so sad for me," the sick woman said in a weary voice, "My time has come, and so I shall soon depart from the world, as must we all. I am content; I have lived fully. I have experienced many joys. And thou, my sweet Alene, have been my greatest joy, along with Jaylinn, though thou were come from my foremost regret, and arrived in this world in my time of greatest sorrow."

Alene looked at her mother with teary eyes, and the words *foremost regret* left her confused.

"My daughter," Elanna continued, "I fear I've not been truthful with thee. I have lived a dreadful lie, and now 'tis time to come clean. Thy father did not die in the Battle of Nemdon before thou were born, but yet lives. For Lord Gregir was not thy true father—I am ashamed to say I was unfaithful to him when he left for battle. And my dear, thy true father is no other than—please be not startled—King Naelor of Minear."

Alene's eyes widened and her face grew pale. She tried to ask further but could not speak.

"Prince Naelor and I knew each other growing up," Lady Elanna continued, "He had ever been interested in me, and I in him. He had come to Tyniad on the orders of King Naygur, his elder brother, just days after my husband went to war, for reasons I can't remember, and we... reconnected." She sighed. "I was foolish back then, young and stupid. I had been terribly lonely, and my mind was haunted with concern for my husband: I needed someone. And Naelor was the right person at the right time. Then, my dear Alene, I began to show signs of pregnancy before too long. And Naelor said to me—I remember his words as if he spoke them yesterday—'You will know the child is mine if it grows to

41

bear any resemblance to me, and if such is the case, you must not reveal to it who its true father is, for I am soon to marry.' And I answered, 'My husband needn't know I've been unfaithful. You have my word.'"

Lady Elanna took a long breath and looked deep into her daughter's eyes as she went on, "He left soon after, and I was alone for a few days before I got the news of my husband's death, and so great was my grief and guilt that I was surprised I didn't miscarry. And I said to myself, 'This child must have quite a destiny.' And my sweet Alene, thou were the most beautiful babe, and as thou grew, I noted that thou indeed bore a strong resemblance to the king. But I never revealed to thee who thou were, for I was bidden not to tell. But my time is about to end, and my gut told me thou needed to learn the truth. I am so sorry, my dear, so very sorry for keeping this from thee for so long. I would forgive thee if thou chose to hate me."

"Oh, Mother," Alene spoke after a pause. "No, I could never hate you. But I will need time for this to sink in. I must go for a walk—by your leave, of course."

Lady Elanna nodded her consent and gave a weak but loving smile. "Certainly, my dear, some fresh air will do thee good."

"Thank you, Mother," Alene responded somewhat distractedly, "I will send for your nurse."

And with that, Lady Alene left her mother's chamber, pale as a ghost, and went down the stairs. As she crossed the marble hallway, she was in such a daze that she did not hear Sir Celgon express his concern for her.

She sent for a nurse to see to Lady Elanna, and exited the stifling castle, stepping out onto the grounds to feel a refreshing breeze brush her face. Walking speedily down the stone pathway between columns of bushes with pink spring roses, Alene considered her mother's words. She could hardly wrap her head around it. She was not a Lady but a Princess, and of *Pevrel* blood. Suddenly, amid her bewilderment and pondering, she was brought back to the present at the call of her name. She turned around to see the nurse hurrying toward her with a grave countenance.

"My Lady," she began, curtseying, "I am ever so sorry, but the Lady Elanna is no more. The sickness got the better of her. But it looks as though she died at ease—she has all the appearance of one who's having a peaceful dream."

Alene felt a harsh pang in her chest. She couldn't believe she'd left her mother's side. She was filled with regret that she had not been there, holding her hand, during her last moments. Her eyes stung and felt uncomfortably dry, but then they welled with tears which trickled down her cheeks. She quickly wiped them away and made her way back to the castle.

She went to her mother, took hold of her dead hand, and kissed it as tears rolled down her cheeks. She then gently brushed her mother's hair from her face and kissed her forehead, then stood up straight and looked upon the woman who raised her single-handedly. Elanna was always so patient with Jaylinn and her. *Jaylinn.* It suddenly made sense now. The sisters, or half-sisters, looked nothing alike. Jaylinn, the elder, aged six-and-twenty, had auburn hair and green eyes, while Alene, aged four-and-twenty, had black hair and dark eyes. They did not look much alike in face, either. Alene sighed. She then went to find her sister to tell her of their mother's passing... And of her parentage...

When Alene told her sister the bad news, the sisters wept together and exchanged some favorite memories of their mother, both tearful, but they managed to share some laughter as well.

Then when Alene revealed that King Naelor was her father, Jaylinn laughed (a reaction that was not unexpected of her sister).

"That explains it, then," Jaylinn said, referring to their contrasting looks. Then she stopped laughing and her face lit up with excitement. "My God, my sister is a *princess*!"

"Oh my," said Alene, realizing how this fact separated her from Jaylinn, and from Tyniad. "I guess I am."

Jaylinn took her sister by the shoulders, a bright smile lighting up her face. "My sister is a *bloody* princess!" She screamed. "Oh my God, Alene, what if thou become queen one day?"

"I imagine I would not," said Alene. "I'm a bastard, arent't I?"

"Well, thou won't be queen with an attitude like that!" Jaylinn laughed again.

"Oh, sister," said Alene, sharing in her laughter. Then after some thought, she said, "I think I'll move to Minear. What think thee?"

"Yes, thou absolutely must," said Jaylinn, her green eyes sparkling.

"Would thou come with me?" Alene asked.

Her sister pouted. "Hmm... eventually, yes." Then, with a smirk, she said, "Right now, I'm having too much fun with Charles and Maevin."

Alene looked downward, laughing. "Oh, sister... is one man not enough for you?"

"Life is short," Jaylinn shrugged. "I might die of consumption yet. If a plague comes for us, I want to be able to die happy."

Alene laughed. "Fair," she said.

"But, sister," Jaylinn spoke. "Thy life is destined to be incredible. Go to Minear. I will soon join thee."

"I shall," Alene decided. Then taking Jaylinn in an embrace, she said, "My beautiful sister... I do hope you'll come to Minear soon."

"Oh, I will," said Jaylinn. "I hear Prince Taelor is quite easy on the eye."

Then after a moment, Alene said, "Oh no, that is my half-brother."

"But he is not *my* half-brother," Jaylinn smirked.

Alene laughed. "Well, goodnight, sister," she said, "I am weary and need my rest."

"Goodnight, Queen Alene," said Jaylinn, curtseying before her sister.

"Oh, don't," Alene chuckled.

The sisters laughed as they departed.

~

Three days after her mother's death, Alene set out on horseback with four knights to travel to Minear, Sir Celgon being the most eager of those selected. It would be a three days' ride.

There were no hardships or attacks along the road from neither beast nor bandit, and there was only one difficult passing along the way, where the terrain was particularly steep and stony. It seemed like fate, as if Alene was destined for Minear. Her heart was glad, and her spirit was high, but her knees still trembled when the great castle came first into sight.

As the company approached closer, they found themselves at a black gate, and there were four guards clad in deep blue vests bearing the silver Pevrel hawk, their bright armor gleaming in the sunlight. They bid Alene's company declare themselves and explain the purpose of their arrival.

"This here is Lady Alene of Tyniad," spoke Sir Celgon, "But that is not her only title, for she has Pevrel blood, also, and is the daughter of none other than your king, the venerable Naelor. We have journeyed thus so that she may introduce herself and unite with her father and take her place here in the fair and prosperous kingdom of Minear."

The guards exchanged glances with each other and resolved to open the gate and let Alene's company pass through. As they approached, the splendor and wonder of the castle began to make Alene feel uneasy. The castle was rounded and smooth, and of a variable gray that appeared as anywhere from silver to coal, depending on the weather and the time of day. At this moment, it was silvery.

At the castle's center, towering higher than all else, was a gigantic and proud hawk of black steel, its wings outspread; and surrounding the castle was a moat, mimicking the circular flight of a hawk once it has eyed its prey. Sir Celgon glanced over at Alene, sensing her nerves, and the two met eyes; he gave her an encouraging nod with a warm smile. A steady confidence spread within her, and she sat up straighter on her horse, adopting the air of a beloved princess returning home. She was of Pevrel blood, *she was a hawk*, and this was her rightful ancestral home.

There were more guards at the castle's entry, and Sir Celgon repeated the words that he spoke at the black gate. Alene's company was ordered to wait outside whilst one guard entered into the castle to inform the king of the visitors. When Naelor was told of the woman waiting outside who claimed to be his daughter, all color drained from his face, though his expression remained neutral.

"Very well," he said, "Let her cross the bridge. Bring her to me."

He summoned his son, Prince Taelor, now two-and-twenty years of age, who was outside training with the knights. The prince's brow wrinkled, and his heart skipped a beat when he was told of the mysterious visitor. With his arm, he wiped the sweat from his forehead and anxiously made his way to the throne room. He stood beside the king, who spoke not a word to him, and the two awaited the presence of the woman in silence.

Alene was brought in, escorted by two Minear guards. When he saw her, Naelor perceived that she resembled him greatly; indeed, she looked more like him than his son did. Taelor resembled his father only in his wavy black hair which reached his shoulders; he had not the strong Pevrel face, but looked like his mother's kin, having inherited her clear and pale complexion, light almond-shaped eyes, the straight nose, and heart-shaped face. Alene, however, looked a typical Pevrel, with the square-shaped face, prominent features, the wide, dark eyes, and the raven hair, which fell in loose waves almost to her hips. She was an attractive woman but had not the captivating beauty that her half-brother so casually possessed.

"Your Grace," Alene began, her voice shaking slightly, "I am come from Tyniad, ever an ally of Minear, to introduce myself. I am the daughter of the Lady Elanna, who passed last week—but before she did, she told me of how you came to be my father. And now that my mother is gone, there is little left for me in Tyniad, so I am come to Minear, to meet you and your son, my half-brother Taelor, and to start anew."

"The Lady Elanna is deceased?" the king asked.

"Yes, Your Grace. She had a fever," Alene answered.

"That is grievous news," said the king. "And very well— I trust that you are my daughter. Your mother was my first love before I married the late Queen Torina. And only a blind man could not see how similar you look to me. I will have a room prepared for you, and you shall become crowned Princess of Minear within the fortnight. Welcome!"

"Thank you, Your Grace," Alene curtseyed.

"*My Liege*, if you would," said Naelor.

"Thank you, My Liege," Alene said.

Prince Taelor was very glad to find out he had a half-sister and was eager to get to know her—however, he tried to conceal this in front of his father who treated the matter quite indifferently.

But that evening when Alene was up in her chamber, enjoying her new room and appreciating the view from her window, a guard entered to tell her she had a visitor: the Prince Taelor. A smile lit up her face, and she said, "Do let him in!"

Prince Taelor walked over to her, appearing slightly nervous as he bowed before her.

"Welcome to Minear," he said, "Who would have thought I had a sister? 'Tis a pleasure."

"'Tis most indeed," agreed Alene, curtseying. "I was quite baffled myself when I found out you were my half-brother."

Taelor smiled. And looking around the room, his eye fell upon a lute propped up on an armchair by the windowsill. Gesturing to it, he said, "Do you play?"

"I do," said Alene happily.

"I've always wanted to play the lute," said Taelor, "But Father would say, *'A prince should be a warrior, not a minstrel; I would sooner see you with sword in hand than lute on lap.'* So I never learned how."

"Perhaps I could teach you sometime," suggested Alene.

"I would like that very much," Taelor smiled.

Alene invited him to sit with her, and the two spoke late into the night. They found that they had much in common: Alene also possessed a love for history, and the two shared many of the same favorite tales of legend. When they finally decided it was time to depart and each go to sleep, the two were gleeful. They had very much enjoyed one another's company and were glad to call each other brother and sister. Alene told Taelor that he was welcome in her chamber any time, and he told her the same.

They met up and spoke for long hours every night for the rest of the week. One stormy evening, with the sound of thunder echoing through the castle, and the piddle of rain sounding upon the window, Alene asked Taelor if he would lean toward justice or mercy once he became ruler.

After some thought, Taelor answered with, "I know not," and his expression was troubled. "Clearly, I will not make a good king."

Alene made him look into her face, and warmly she said, "There thou art wrong, for a good king must be wise, and a wise king does not fixate on one or the other, but judges each circumstance accordingly, listening to those around him."

But Taelor said, "I do not want to become king. The prospect troubles me. Sometimes I have nightmares about sitting on the throne and making all the wrong decisions whilst Minear crumbles around me. And then other times I cannot sleep all the night, for fear of being a bad monarch."

Alene felt pity for her brother. "Thou art yet young," she said, "and King Naelor has many years before him. Thou need not worry. Thou wilt become wiser with age, and if I may say so, thou art already wise beyond thy years. And thy fear of making a decision that would lead Minear into peril only proves that thou art free of rashness. History shows that rash, thoughtless kings are sooner to bring destruction upon their country than the self-doubting ones."

In a small voice, Taelor said, "Father once told me I would be a weak king."

Alene thought this a nasty thing for any parent to say to their child, and responded, "Why ever would he say that?"

Taelor sighed. "About a year ago, during a council, Father was strategizing war upon the kingdom of Laiden because he felt that King Sederr was taking advantage of the trade system, that Laiden's goods were taxed higher than Minear's, and when my father raised the tax on Minear's goods, Sederr responded with making Laiden's even higher. But I thought it a foolish reason to start a war and spoke out at the council. But Father's mind would not be swayed, and he grew angry and condemned me weak, and said if I do not harden up, I will become a weak king and bring Minear to ruin. Perhaps he is right…"

His confession of birthright-induced fear brought Taelor back to the time in the gallery of portraits when he stood with his Uncle Nadir, looking upon their ancestors. They stopped in front of the portrait of Naygur; first son of Gedur, the pride and joy of his father, and elder brother to Naelor and Nadir. Nadir was much closer to Naygur than Naelor ever was, due mostly to the fact that their relationship was not tainted with rivalry or bitterness, both of which were purely on Naelor's end. For that reason, as well as the fact that Naelor dealt with grief coldly and quietly, Taelor seldom heard the name Naygur pass his father's lips.

Very comely was the painted figure, wavy black hair just slightly short of hanging about the deep blue of his tunic, the proud hawk of shining silver on his breast. Naygur's face was immensely more handsome than Naelor or Nadir's, and as Taelor looked into the painted eyes, so lifelike and expressive were they, he almost felt as if Naygur were there with him.

But Naygur died long before Taelor was born. So nervous was Naygur about becoming king, Nadir had said, that by the time it happened, the burden was so great to bear that Naygur fell into a helpless darkness. He had accidentally started a war with the small island of Crole, where Taelor's mother was to come from. Crole's army slaughtered its way from Minear's outskirts to the heart of Minear, the castle. One night, Naygur put poison in his own chalice of wine and passed the kingship over to Naelor with his death. Naygur was five-and-twenty and Naelor three-and-twenty. King Naelor put an end to the war, and in an act of peacemaking, married a princess of Crole, Torina of House Cotter, whose magnificent beauty made Naelor the luckiest king to ever attain the throne through the suicide of his elder brother.

As Taelor looked into the portrait's dark eyes that the artist had so skillfully captured the youthful touch of restless impatience within, it seemed hard for Taelor to believe that Naygur would take his own life. And the stories that Nadir told of Naygur, who was closer to him than anyone, made it all the harder to believe, for these stories painted a young man of great mirth and exuberance. Nadir told his nephew how much all the girls loved Naygur, but that information was unnecessary after having seen his portrait, yet Nadir did not hold back to tell Taelor of how his deceased uncle would bed a different girl practically every night. Nadir shook his head at this, smiling slightly to himself. Naygur behaved in ways that embarrassed Nadir, yet Nadir always described Naygur as a good young man, and the most loving and supportive brother a young boy could ask for. Nadir then wiped his eyes with a sleeve and bid Taelor farewell, departing with his head hung low. And Taelor continued looking upon the portrait of Naygur, sensing a strange bond over the shared fear of ruling a kingdom.

Then tearing away from these thoughts, Taelor came back to the present and looked over to see his half-sister staring at him; her expression was full of confusion.

"Taelor?" she spoke, her voice holding concern.

Then Taelor, wishing to evade speaking further of his troubles, said, "Dost thou still hold to the offer of teaching me to play the lute?"

"Of course," said Alene.

Taelor, though troubled, smiled as best as he could muster, and bid his sister goodnight.

The next day, when the sun began to sink in the sky, Taelor made his way to his sister's chamber once again.

He asked Alene if she would first play for him a song, for he had not yet heard her strum upon the lute, to which

Alene was glad to oblige. She played a cheerful tune, and her fingers as they moved on the neck of the lute, or plucked at the strings, were like little birds spreading wing, and her voice as she sang was like the clear blue sky they flew in. Taelor did not know whether it was merely for the love he bore his sister, but this melody and performance seemed to him the most beautiful thing he had ever heard.

When her song ended, Taelor was speechless. Then Alene handed the lute over to him and began teaching him the basics. Once he had half-way mastered the first thing she taught him, his face lit up. "I can play!" he said, his manner childlike.

Alene laughed kindly and said, "Well, not quite yet. But this is a start!"

Excitedly he asked her to teach him more.

By the end of the night, Taelor could play a simple tune, and he was merrier than he had been in many a year. He did not want for the music lesson to end, but Alene was tired, so they said farewell, and Alene promised they would continue the next day.

Taelor walked back to his own chamber, a smile still playing on his lips. Upon entering, he saw that his servant, Leygon, was in the room, rummaging through a basket by the wall.

"Well, hello!" Taelor blurted, rather startled.

"Hi, Taelor," said Leygon. "Sorry, I've misplaced my belt. I know not where 'tis gone to."

"Surely you need it not for sleeping?" said Taelor.

"No," answered Leygon. "But I will in the morn." Leygon was such a little thing; a belt was essential to fasten his trousers about his tiny waist. He was short of stature, and if he were any skinner, he would certainly appear ill. He had a good appetite, though; Leygon always surprised Taelor with how much he could eat. And likewise, Taelor surprised Leygon with how much wine he could drink. Leygon did not have a taste for wine, which Taelor could not understand.

Taelor went over to his chest of drawers and retrieved one of his own belts. "Will this do for now?" he asked, handing it to Leygon.

"It will," said Leygon appreciatively, "Much nicer than mine, too. Thanks."

"Thou art quite welcome," answered Taelor.

Leygon smiled. "Where were you anyway, so late at night? I was sure you'd be in your chambers by this hour."

"My sister was teaching me to play the lute," said Taelor.

"You've been wanting to learn how to play, haven't you?"

"I have," said Taelor, "But my father always preferred me to practice my swordsmanship."

"Silly, really," said Leygon, "because a lute not only makes music but also makes for a pretty fine weapon if you clobber someone over the head with it."

Taelor gazed at his servant questioningly, not wanting to show signs of amusement.

"Well, it would," Leygon defended himself. "Imagine if you were armed with a lute at the Battle of the Green Field."

"Art thou drunk this night? I would not have killed many men," said Taelor, grinning slightly.

"No, but you would have knocked out quite a few! How many men did you kill in that battle anyway?"

"More than I care to think with my crossbow. One with my sword."

"Just one with your sword? Perhaps you would have done better with a lute," teased Leygon.

Taelor smirked despite himself. "Answer me this, Leygon: would thou care to be added to the list of men I have killed?"

"Not particularly," admitted Leygon with a chuckle, "And look at that, 'tis my bedtime! On the morrow!"

But the morning proved foul, for King Naelor had grown contemptuous toward Alene's presence and felt aggrieved at Taelor's fondness of her. Moreover, his mind had become ever more concerned with Alene's birthright. Was she to remain princess, or would she, being the elder of his two children, be next in line to the throne? Therefore, he spoke with Mr. Catan, an old advisor and the keeper of records. Mr. Catan had to delve in thorough research on the matter, for no incident like this had yet occurred in the history of Minear. Alene's illegitimacy and having been brought up in a different kingdom, by a different House, brought multiple concerns to question.

After Mr. Catan had read through many a scripture, he told the king to his immense dismay that Alene would, in fact, be his heir, not Taelor. Alene was two years Taelor's senior, and although she was a bastard, her mother was of the highly regarded House Loring which had a long history of alliance with House Pevrel, as the House of Taelor's mother did not.

Naelor thought this ridiculous, yet he disguised his malice and forced composure upon his features. In his greedy heart, he would not have a woman follow him on the throne, especially not after believing for two-and-twenty years that Taelor would be his successor—a man, who would secure the name of Pevrel in kingship of Minear. Indeed, Naelor would not see the Pevrel dynasty meet its end. He could not let Alene succeed him.

In the dark of night, he called upon two trusty assassins and ordered them to fix numerous trapped arrows with poisoned tips in Alene's room the day following, whilst she was out taking her morning walk.

So came the following day. Around noon, after her walk, Alene went up to her chamber to change her gown. But as she opened the wardrobe door, an arrow pierced her left arm, just below the elbow. She screamed a frightful scream, and the effect of the poison made her vision hazy and her body weak, so she laid herself on the floor. Two guards entered upon her scream, and taking Alene in their arms, they brought her to the healing house. The nurses and court physician, Bengir, drew the poison and gathered herbs to lift the fever. Her heart rate became steadier and her complexion less pallid, but still she lay unconscious, her body cold to the touch, her face clammy.

When Taelor heard of this some hour hence, he rushed to the healing room in a great panic, a crushing feeling in his chest, which increased with each stride. He entered the room and found his half-sister lying seemingly lifeless upon one of the beds, and so much did she remind him of his mother when she was dying from her illness, that he fell onto his knees beside her and grabbed her hand, weeping.

"As fair as a flower, and as warm as the sunshine that sees to its blooming," he said, "Yet oft does even the strongest flower wither before winter's close... Alas that one so sweet should perish before her time." And looking upon her face, he cried, "No, I cannot lose thee! My sweet sister."

He got up from his knees and kissed Alene's brow, one of his tears falling on her forehead.

Then from the other side of the room, a soft and kindly voice spoke, "My, you do jump to conclusions, young prince! And you are quite the pessimist, yet also quite a poet!"

Taelor, believing he was alone with Alene, jumped at the sound of the voice, which belonged to Bengir, the court physician. The thin man with graying hair sat on a chair in the corner, obscured in shadow. He rose and walked over to where Taelor was standing.

Gazing down upon his patient, Bengir spoke, "Nay, young prince, she is not dying. She is on the mend. The poison has been drawn, and the nurses have used a selection of herbs on her. We have seen great improvement in her, and she will wake before too long. You need not worry, Prince, you are not losing your half-sister!"

Taelor felt as if the weight of all the world's grief was lifted from his back.

"I thank you!" was all he could say, dazed by the shock and grief, followed by sudden relief. He made his way back up to his chamber and sat at his desk.

Still, as he sat, he wondered who would have done such a thing to his sister. Someone in Minear wanted her dead. He wondered who it could have been. And the outcome of all his reasoning pointed to his father. He resented Alene's arrival in Minear, Taelor could tell; and the proud Naelor did not want a daughter, especially one older than his son. And Taelor, being of sharp mind, perceived that the king must have discovered that it was Alene's birthright, not his, to sit on Minear's throne (which Taelor had already guessed, and not begrudged). It all added up. He had no doubt that this attempt at murder was his father's doing. Immense anger welled inside him, and a shadow of evil altered his fair face.

He stood from his seat, grabbed his sword, Luin, and sheathed it at his hip, then headed to the throne room, his face hard and his eyes cold.

King Naelor gasped when the doors of the hall were so violently flung open. Taelor came storming in, noting there was not a single guard in sight. Naelor looked like a dark shadow in a haze of gray and deep blue. But even from this distance, Taelor could not mistake the air of guilt and fear. Naelor had clearly sent the guards away for the sake of solitude so that none could have the chance to read his troubled mind.

"You meant to have my half-sister killed, didn't you, Father?" Taelor yelled, drawing his sword, his right hand tight around the hilt.

"I—I did it for thee, my son," Naelor stumbled.

"For me?" Taelor spat. "Oh yes, take the life of she who is dearest to me, just so I can take the throne I do not want, to save your precious Pevrel dynasty from meeting its end!"

"Taelor, thou art riled. Go to thy chamber. I can send for Leygon to bring thee wine."

"Wine? I do not want wine!" Taelor boomed, "I want justice! Pick up your sword, Father!"

Naelor grew pale. "I will not fight my son," he said in a soft but sturdy tone.

"Well, then I will just have to strike you down defenseless!"

"You would not," said Naelor, coolly enough.

"You underestimate me, Father. I would for what you have done! Perhaps I do have some of your ruthlessness in my blood, after all!"

"Taelor, calm thyself," said Naelor, becoming more unnerved.

Taelor just stood there, his glance stern and his mind unchanging. "Father, pick up your sword," he hissed through clenched teeth.

Naelor did not move, but all color drained from his face.

"Father, will you die unarmed at my mercy, or will you die fighting with sword in hand?"

Naelor drew an exasperated breath. Defeated, he picked up his sword from the desk beside him, and the two began to duel.

Naelor was fighting only in defense, but Taelor had a wildfire surging in him and was fighting for the kill. Tears welled treacherously in Naelor's eyes, blurring his vision as he blocked each of Taelor's vicious strikes, the clanging of their swords echoing off the vast stone walls and ceiling, their boots squeaking against the cold marble floor.

Taelor was tireless, his adrenaline flowing. But Naelor was becoming slow, weakened by his son's violence toward him and by his seven-and-forty years of age. Finally, worn down and full of despair, he sprang away and held his sword down at his side.

"Taelor, please," he begged desperately through short breaths.

Taelor met his father's gaze, and Naelor saw that his son's face was still hard and that his eyes still looked at him like a predator after his prey.

"Forgive me, my son," Naelor continued.

Taelor's expression was unchanging, yet he stood still.

Naelor, exhausted, and feeling like Taelor would now come to his senses, flung down his sword, the dull clang of steel meeting marble piercing both father and son's ears, and fell onto his knees.

Taelor slowly and calmly strode toward his father, sword out in front of him, and he held the point to the king's throat. Naelor looked up to meet his son's eyes, and the king's face showed mingled disbelief and betrayal.

"You would not slay me," Naelor said, trying to sound calm. "Not only am I your father and your king, but also I am unarmed and wearied and defenseless; I have taught you better."

A cruel smirk curved Taelor's lips, and he replied in a bitter voice, "There you are wrong, Father. In both things. I *will* indeed slay you, and nay, you have not taught me better, for just before you would have killed my half-sister, your own daughter, whilst she was defenseless."

Naelor sobbed. "Please, my son ... Forgive me..."

"Forgive you?" Taelor mocked, his sword still pointed at his father's throat, "Is that what you would have said if your attempt at assassination were successful? If life were gone from Alene's body and she became cold and white, soon to rot under the earth? 'Forgive me?'" Taelor stared down at his father with severity. "Your reign is ended, Father, and the line of Pevrel will hold the throne no longer. It has all come to a bitter end."

Tears were streaming down Naelor's face, and he suddenly looked no longer like an aging king, but an abandoned child. The sight of his father like this cooled Taelor's temper for a moment, and his heart was softened. He lowered his sword from the king's throat, but still pointed it toward him, although his grip was loosened. The point hovered around the king's chest, and as Naelor looked into Taelor's eyes, he still saw vengeful fury on the edge of madness glint in them and was frightened.

In a wild, desperate attempt to break free from Taelor with his life, he brought up his right hand and grabbed the blade, holding it still. Crimson blood appeared around

Naelor's firm grip and came trickling down the blade, dripping onto the floor. Taelor watched the blood and heard the *drip* on the marble, finding it grotesque. And indeed this sight made Taelor's initial intention truly sink in. He had meant to murder his father but was unsure whether he could do it. Becoming hyper-aware of his stance and the feel of the hilt of Luin in his hand, his mind became hazy, and he felt as if he were dreaming some vile dream.

But as he looked once again into his father's face, and memories of his few but precious moments with Alene came flooding through his mind, the fire within him raged once more. Naelor would have ended that, would have taken Alene from him. Moreover, he would have taken an innocent life, killed a woman—a woman who also happened to be his own daughter. It seemed Naelor had no conscience. Taelor concluded that a man such as this deserved death. But could he be the one who dealt it to him? His mind said no, that, of course, he had it not in his blood to commit patricide. But his heart which burned with the love he bore his half-sister, and his soul that was fueled with rage, screamed *yes*. In fact, he believed he should be the one to avenge Alene.

"You *disgust* me," Taelor said as he looked down at Naelor.

"Yet it is you holding his father at sword point, watching as he bleeds," said Naelor.

"That is of your own doing," said Taelor, "This whole scene is of your own doing."

Naelor could no longer find a voice.

Taelor's grip on the hilt tightened once again. With narrowed eyes, he said, "Have you any last words, Father?"

"Yes," Naelor struggled, "That thou art my son."

Uncontrollable tears began to rise in Taelor's eyes. But then his countenance became repulsed, and he said, "No, I am not your son. There is nothing of you in me. Nothing."

"Thou *art* my son," said Naelor, "As thou always have been, as thou always wilt be. And I am proud to call thee such. Sheath thy sword, Taelor."

"I cannot be your son," Taelor said venomously, and his arm jerked as he said it.

Startled by this sudden movement, Naelor's left hand grabbed the blade, as well as his right. But in his fear, he used too much force, and Taelor, whose grasp on the hilt was firm and whose legs were weak from all he was feeling, was thrown off balance. He came falling forward and collapsed onto his father. As he struggled to his feet and looked down at Naelor, he saw that the blade was plunged deep into his father's lower chest, and an ever-growing patch of blood surrounded the wound. Taelor's crazed eyes met his father's, and he saw that they were lifeless.

He fell onto his knees beside his father and scanned his face, mouth agape and hands trembling. He could not believe what he had done. No sound could pass his lips, and for a moment, he could not arise. Time seemed to stand completely still as he looked upon the dead king.

~

Taelor could not sleep at all the night he killed his father, nor the second, nor the third - until at last, just moments before the sun rose, he drifted off. But his subconscious taunted him by making him relive the moment of murdering Naelor, twisting and exaggerating the scene. Taelor jerked awake, his heart racing, and he saw the image of his father standing at his bedside, a gory ghost looking down upon him with eyes sinister and haunting. Taelor let out a blood-curdling scream, causing the horrid likeness of his father to slip away.

A guard appeared moments after, and Taelor stared at him with crazy eyes, his pasty face gleaming in a cold sweat. The guard then, realizing that the prince must have had a nightmare and that no one had broken in, coldly turned away and left the room. Taelor lay back down, trembling wildly beneath his bedsheets. He soon fell asleep once more and became lost in deep slumber. His servant, Leygon, knowing of the prince's sleeplessness, did not wake him until after noon, and Taelor's first thought when he awoke from that deep slumber was that killing the king had been but an evil nightmare. And for a hopeful moment that is all he thought it was, but then the harsh reality dawned on him, and he suddenly felt sick. A hateful shadow of despair sought to suffocate him in his grief, and he fell to the ground, cursing his very nature, while Leygon stood beside him, hopeless and miserable.

The next week came like chill weather after a heavy storm, the mood drab and gloomy. Alene was now in full health, and she became queen, and Nadir became her counselor. Taelor thought Alene's first days on the throne admirable; yet, despite his love and respect for his half-sister, he could not bear to see her on the throne. His whole life, he had known his father on that throne, and seeing Alene rule in his place was a cruel reminder of how he had killed him. And unlike Alene who had already gained the love of the people and the court, though they still mourned for their late king, all of Minear had turned on Taelor. Many could not look at him, and others yelled "Killer of Father" or "Slayer of King" after him. He had fallen into a great state of dishonor, and they all believed him black of heart, a very instrument of the devil. Not only did he commit murder and treason, but the blood of a parent was on his hands. They all despised him, yet not one of them half as much as he despised himself.

His days were torturous, and his nights were worse. On one evening, while in his chamber, he unsheathed his sword Luin, and said, "The blade that took my father shall now take me; thus justice will be paid," and pointed the sword to his abdomen. For a moment, he stood thus, but he could not plunge the sword into his belly. Although he did not want to live, neither did he want to die. Plus, this would not be a swift death like what he had granted his father, yet what choice did he have? It would be near impossible to stab himself through the heart. This was the only way; he could not die instantly, but in agony. He heard his own voice repeating in his mind, cold as the moon, cruel as lightning, that it was no more than he deserved. Then he began to weep, his body shaking all over, and he dropped his sword, fell onto the floor, and lay there curled up and trembling. It was like this that Leygon found him.

Acknowledging the presence of his servant, Taelor spoke shakily, "I could not do it, Leygon. Yet I fear not death. Nay, only the pain of dying. But I want it to be over. I abhor my very skin! I killed my own father! But he would have seen Alene murdered in cold blood! Nonetheless, I can't go on, Leygon. My heart is plagued with evil. It is blackened. Please, Leygon, wilt thou end me, as duty to thy master?"

Picking up his sword from the floor beside him, Taelor faced the hilt toward Leygon, and the blue gems set in it gleamed in the candlelight like fireflies. But Leygon would not grab the hilt, and just looked upon Taelor as one whose heart might break.

"Taelor, please," Leygon spoke at last. "This is not you—you are not a murderer. Stop this self-loathing. You have a good heart. And your father deserved what he got—"

"He was thy king!" Taelor snapped, "Thou speak treason! Talk not such disrespect, thou degraded servant!"

Leygon stared in surprise, this outburst leaving him at a loss for words. Taelor had never spoken to him like this; he had always spoken to him as a dear friend.

Taelor then looked into Leygon's boyish face, and it pained him to see it like this, bereft of its usual cheerfulness, as it had been since Naelor's death.

"I am sorry, Leygon," he said, "I did not mean to—Thou art right, I am not myself. But I never will be again. I am tainted. So is my sword. It thirstily drank the blood of my father, and now it is fitting that it should drink mine."

Leygon knelt beside Taelor.

"Would you listen to yourself?" Leygon asked. "Come, now… If you were to die, yes, you would no longer feel the grief that is troubling you. But you would also prevent your many opportunities of the future from coming to be. Do not lose hope, Taelor—you can redeem yourself. There is still so much in the world for you. Do not wish to end your life when so many who wish to live die from illness or are slain..." Leygon fumbled with his fingers, and looking down at his hands, he saw that they were trembling. "And not only would you end your own life, but you would destroy other people's as well," Leygon continued. "Your half-sister loves you very much. It would kill her to see you dead. And so it would me. You are my dearest friend, Taelor…"

Tears flooded from Taelor's eyes. "You say there is still much in the world for me," he said, "But how can that be so? What hope can one wish for who has killed one's own father? Nay, there is nothing for me. Only darkness…"

"There is never only darkness," answered Leygon, "Light always manages to shine through, somehow. And light overpowers darkness. For even the tiniest light can lift darkness, whereas a little darkness makes no hindrance to light."

Taelor's mood was lifted slightly.

Leygon gave a small smile. "Please, Taelor," he continued, "Believe me that there is as much hope for you as for any. And do you not want to live? Just for the sake of being alive? To go out and feel the warmth of the sun on your skin, or the cool breeze chilling your bones, or the fresh air brushing against your face and ruffling through your hair? To hear the birds sing, and to just exist in this wonderful world we were brought into?"

Tears streamed down Taelor's cheeks once more, but this time because he was moved. He had never known Leygon to be either deep or poetic, and the words that Leygon spoke indeed gave him a new outlook. Taelor no longer foresaw only darkness. He arose and sat up next to Leygon yet did not look at him.

"Thou hast swayed me," Taelor said, "Yet, I think, Leygon, that I must go. I must leave Minear and never return. If there is hope for me in this world, it is not here. If I am to remain in Minear, I will surely drown in darkness." After a pause, he continued, "I see now that I must exile myself and forsake my title. To fashion myself anew." He took a deep breath, and then he again spoke, "I will relieve thee from thy servanthood, Leygon. And I will give thee gold in plenty, to thank thee for all thou hast done."

Leygon grinned widely to see Taelor come around, and a glint shone in his bright blue eyes as he answered, "Are you quite serious? You are my friend, Taelor, and where you go, I will go willingly."

Touched by Leygon's loyalty, tears filled Taelor's eyes once again. "So be it," he struggled, his heart welling inside him.

Leygon gave Taelor a gentle pat on the back, and the two continued to sit on the floor for some moments, in comfortable silence.

~

The next day, before noon, Taelor visited Alene and asked if he could speak to her in private. And with a concerned expression, Alene said, "Of course," and she sent out the guards and closed the doors of the throne room.

"Tomorrow, I am leaving Minear, for good," Taelor said.

Alene looked shocked and pained. After a moment she said, "Is it because of the people? I have told them to stop taunting thee, and I can be stricter on them—I can start putting them in a cell if they dare utter 'Killer of Father' or 'Slayer of King.' Would thou stay then?"

Taelor sighed. "My sweet sister, I am afraid it is more than that. I killed my father. Minear has become nightmarish to me. I must get away."

Alene was deeply saddened, yet her glance conveyed warmth and understanding. She nodded her head gravely. "Then leave thou must," she said weakly.

Taelor gently cradled her head in his hands and kissed her forehead. "I will miss thee more than I have ever missed anyone."

"We have only just gotten to know each other," she said sadly, the natural sweetness of her voice accentuated by her sorrow.

"I know," said Taelor, "I wish it need not be this way." He smiled the best he could, and Alene invited him to dine with her that night.

When evening came, the two half-siblings feasted together. It was a shame that, due to the occasion, so grand a meal could not be fully enjoyed. And though sweet and plentiful was the wine, the atmosphere was drab and mirthless. Hardly a word was spoken between Alene and Taelor, for fear of tears—yet just being in each other's company, one last time, was enough for the both of them.

Once they had finished their food and drunk their share of wine, the time came for farewells. They fell into each other's arms and stood in an embrace for a long moment.

Then at last when they separated, Alene said, "Take me with thee," her voice barely audible.

Taelor was confused. "But thou art queen."

Alene smiled gently. "Nay," she said, "I meant, take me with thee in here," and she laid her hand upon his chest.

"My sweet sister, thou knowest thou hast my heart."

Alene began to sob, and Taelor's eyes were so filled with tears that all he could see of his half-sister was the outline of her form. Then he grabbed her hand and kissed it and looked into her face one last time before he turned to leave forever.

Chapter 5: The Outlaws and the Phantom

Dawn came with a sky of gray. The sun was obscured, but the cheerless rays pierced through the masses of wispy clouds. Leygon awoke Taelor, who moaned and squinted his eyes against the rays of light from the window and rolled over. Leygon pulled the covers from him gently and said, "Well, today is the day."

Taelor groaned and sat up, staring out ahead at nothing in particular. Leygon handed him a cup of hot chocolate, and Taelor sipped at it. He looked over at Leygon, who was now setting up his breakfast on the desk near the foot of his bed.

"How art thou feeling?" Taelor asked.

"About leaving Minear?" answered Leygon, "Well... I know not what to feel yet. 'Tis strange. But quite exciting, in a way."

Taelor grinned feebly.

"We'll put this in the past," said Leygon, referring to Naelor's death. "We'll begin something new, and things will get better. You will get better."

Before Leygon left Taelor's chamber to give his master some privacy, he gazed about the room. He felt a strange sense of loss as he looked around, and he walked to the door with heavy feet.

~

Once Taelor had finished breakfast, clothed himself in plain brown fabrics and leathers, and prepared a bag of things to bring along on his travels (including a couple of changes of clothing, two water skins, some freshly baked bread for the road, and a crossbow with a supply of arrows), he called for Leygon.

The two then headed to the court blacksmith's smithy, as was planned. Taelor abandoned his sword Luin, for he could no longer bear the sword he used to slay his father, and in his despair, he cursed it and believed it to be tainted. Also, it was too ornate for the mere knight he was now to fashion himself. Luin was indeed a prince's sword, and Taelor had once greatly admired its beauty—the blade was long and elegant, the craftsmanship in the hilt exquisite, and the blue gems set in it twinkled and shined in all lightings. He had named it Luin after the Elvish word for "blue," the long-forgotten language of the wise, immortal people from the lore he loved to read. Under different circumstances, Taelor would have grieved to part with Luin, but now he was only too relieved.

He would also not start on his journey with Leygon unless he, too, was armed, inexperienced with a blade though he was. So in the smithy, the blacksmith let both Taelor and Leygon handle all the swords they took an interest in. Leygon found one that he was satisfied with quickly, but Taelor was fussy, and he tried out many before finding one that he liked. It was much plainer a sword than what he was used to, but as he swung it, he found that it felt similar to Luin, and he was comfortable wielding it.

The blacksmith smiled at Taelor and said, "A good choice. 'Tis the finest of my current selection, one of the best I've ever forged!"

"I doubt it not," said Taelor, "'Tis a fine blade."

Taelor handed the blacksmith a bag of gold, watching as his eyes lit up.

"One of my finest crafts as it is, still it cannot be worth this prize!" said the blacksmith, in awe at the wealth Taelor handed him.

"'Tis for both my sword and my companion's," said Taelor.

"I still would not have dared expect such a price, Sire!" said the blacksmith.

"No need to call me 'Sire,' I am afraid," Taelor said. "I resign all titles. I am to leave Minear. I am not a prince; I am just a man." And sheathing his new sword, he turned to leave. But as he turned, he saw his uncle, Prince Nadir, standing there looking at him.

"Uncle!" he blurted.

"Your gracefulness is almost humbling, nephew," Nadir said. "I am come because I know thou art fleeing Minear. I dreamt it. I am come to bid thee farewell, but my heart tells me 'tis not a farewell of a forever kind, as thou may think, Taelor."

Taelor was touched and relieved that his uncle still had love for him.

"I resent thy deed, Taelor," said Nadir, "But thou art still my nephew, and I am overall proud of the man I have watched you become. As for thy father, well, I always knew he would get what he had coming. His attempt to murder your sister is unspeakable. A tyrant I knew him, but I knew him not so despicable so to try at the life of his own blood, an innocent woman…"

Taelor had no sufficient response, and his throat was now too tight to speak.

"I would have made an effort to visit thee, Taelor," continued Nadir, "but I needed time. I hope my ignoring thee did not lead thee to believe I no longer cared."

Taelor put his arms around Nadir, taking him in an embrace.

"I understand, Uncle," he said. "I thank you for seeing me off."

"I would not let my only nephew depart without my goodbye and well wishes," Nadir said.

When they released each other, Taelor said, "Take care of Alene!"

"I will," said Nadir, "She is a fine woman, and makes an admirable queen. Thou must be proud to call her thy sister."

"I am very proud," said Taelor. Then his eyes welled with tears, and he turned away from Nadir with a nod of his head. Approaching Leygon, he laid a hand on his back. "Let us be off," he said.

"Taelor!" Nadir called from behind.

Taelor turned. "Yes, Uncle?"

"Thou did not think I'd let thee go off with just thy manservant, did thee?" he smiled somewhat oddly. "Nay. There are two knights waiting outside, Sir Lance and Sir Gavin. They will accompany thee."

"Oh. Well, thank you, Uncle." Then after a pause, Taelor said, "I really will miss you, Uncle."

"Thou wilt not have to miss me for long," said Nadir, his odd smile appearing on his face again.

A little confused, Taelor just gave his uncle a last small nod of his head before turning away.

Taelor and Leygon headed out into the cool morning air. It was crisp against their faces, and the soft wind danced in their hair. Sir Lance and Sir Gavin were there waiting for them, standing beside two brown horses and Taelor's own beautiful horse, Minny. If the former Prince Taelor were to have picked a handful of knights to represent Minear, neither Lance nor Gavin would have been chosen. They were unkempt, middle-aged men with crass manners, and Gavin was an infamous drunkard. But Lance, Taelor had to admit, was a great swordsman.

"Well, where are we going?" Lance asked happily as if this was a trip for pleasure and Taelor hadn't just murdered his own father, their king.

"Away," answered Taelor, mounting Minny. Leygon could not ride, and Taelor pulled him up onto Minny, behind him.

"Oh, now that's a pairing!" Lance exclaimed as Leygon put his arms around Taelor, visibly nervous about being on a horse. "Might I say you make a lovely couple!"

"Last I heard he's shagging his half-sister," said Gavin.

Lance looked at Gavin astonished and gave him a brisk nudge.

Taelor did not respond, but his eyes showed exactly how he felt.

The knights mounted their horses, and Taelor set off with them following behind. They were heading southeast. In a few days, they would reach Tyniad.

"So, we're going to Tyniad?" asked Lance.

"Yes," answered Taelor.

"Then how about, after a lodging there, we sail the sea to the islands of Espuilida?" Lance suggested. "I've always wanted to go! Gorgeous islands, and the women are even more gorgeous, so I hear!"

"Maybe," said Taelor.

"Maybe the women are more gorgeous, or maybe we'll go?" asked Lance.

"Maybe we'll go."

"You wouldn't be seeing me again, boys!" said Gavin, "I'd be in a big bed with the island's most beautiful women."

Taelor doubted it. Gavin must have a lot of gold because only gold could possibly persuade a woman to sleep with him. He was a stout, bulky man with a big, bald, sweaty head and a bright red pimply face.

"I'll be lazing on the beach," said Lance, "under a palm tree, with my arms around two gorgeous gals." Lance was a rather plain man himself, with small light blue eyes above a big, bumpy nose. Lank brown hair hung to the length of his stubbly chin.

"I burn and flake in the sun," said Gavin, "I'm just interested in their women and wine."

"Espuilidian women and Espuilidian wine are the two finest things in this world," Lance sang, "But first we'll have to settle for Tyniadan women... I'm sure Tyniad has its share of beauties as well."

"Any women are fine by me, as long as I get them," said Gavin.

Taelor, irked, snapped, "Do you always talk about women in this manner? And are women *all* you two ever talk about?"

"No," said Lance, "We're knights. Sometimes we talk about swords, too."

"And where we'd like to stick ours!" chortled Gavin.

Taelor stopped his horse. Lance and Gavin stopped theirs as well.

"If I hear one more piece of vulgarity from you, Gavin," Taelor said, "I swear I'll stick my sword in your throat."

"Oh, like you did your half-sister, eh?" Gavin snickered.

Lance shook his head incredulously.

"Leave!" Taelor snapped, anger welling inside him. "Away with you! I don't want to see you again! Lance, you stay."

Gavin reluctantly turned to leave, galloping back toward the castle.

"That idiot's mouth will get him in big trouble one day," said Lance.

"You would do well to watch your mouth, too, Lance. If you weren't one of the best swordsmen I've seen, perhaps I'd be sending you away as well."

Lance was wise enough not to give a reply.

The road from Minear to Tyniad was a plain one. The land was mostly flat, sometimes green, other times brown. It was a rather barren road and an easy one to pass. Taelor was relieved that the city around the castle of Minear was on the north side. He felt that if they had passed through the city, the people would have thrown fruit at him.

"My name is now Tev," Taelor remembered to tell Lance.

"Oh, right," said Lance. "And is my name now Lev?"

Taelor was unamused. "Well, I'm not going to keep my prince name, am I?

"So you came up with Tev?"

"What's wrong with it?" Taelor asked.

"Nothing," Lance decided to say, "'Tis as good a name as any."

They rode on as the pale morning sky grew steadily brighter. After an hour or so of riding, Lance announced that he needed to "heed the call of nature," warning that he'd be a while. He wandered a ways off.

Lance was some minutes gone when Taelor took out the baked bread from his bag and broke some off to eat. He offered some to Leygon who ate it hungrily. Once their energy was replenished, Taelor took the opportunity to teach Leygon some basic combat moves. He didn't like the thought of Leygon being defenseless; being armed with a sword was useless unless he knew how to use it.

They each drew their swords and Taelor tried to get Leygon to master the footwork and motion necessary for blocking. Leygon tried very hard to get his movements right, but he struggled, and Taelor was surprisingly tough on him. When Lance reappeared, Leygon was relieved to break away from Taelor. Leygon sat himself on the hard ground, catching his breath, his cheeks a bright pink. He put his left hand to his right bicep and frowned. "Swords are so heavy," he said, "My arm feels like it shall fall quite off."

Taelor sat down next to his friend. "That is thy arm getting strong," he said warmly. Then laying a hand on Leygon's shoulder, he said, "We will ride again when thou art ready."

Some moments later, the three took off once more. They journeyed on until the westward sun grew big and bright. They were all quite hungry, and Lance wouldn't stop going on about a smoked ham. They rode just a couple of miles further and soon enough, as the sun set and wild violets and oranges filled the sky, they arrived at the city of Gitbury, near the border of Tyniad.

Taelor put on the brown hood of his cloak and gazed about. It was unlikely that he should be recognized here, but he feared it nonetheless. Then suddenly he heard a man call out to them from behind, and, startled, he turned around to see a tall man in regal attire. Taelor let out a ghastly scream, for this man had the face of his late father. And if the man's face did not then change, Taelor's eyes must have refocused, because now he saw that this man was not his father, nor a king, but just an ordinary fellow in a shabby old coat. The color came back to Taelor's face, and he composed himself. Leygon looked at him with concern.

"Why, I apologize to have scared you, chap! But I suppose mine is not the most pleasant of faces!" The man belted a hoarse laugh. "I was only wondering if you and your friends were lost. You don't seem like locals."

"We… Uh… No, we are not. We are visiting some old friends," said Taelor. "We arranged to meet at the inn. Perhaps you can help us find it?"

"Well, which one, boy?" barked the man, "There's The Hairy Horse, The Tiger's Tail, The Big Bull and the Hatted Hare, The Sly Squirrel, The Hunter's Hut, The— "

"We're supposed to be meeting in the biggest one," interrupted Leygon.

"The biggest one, eh?" said the man, "Well, which one is the biggest?" he asked himself, scratching his bearded chin and looking downward in thought. "It's got to be The Big Bull and the Hatted Hare. Aye, I think so."

"Great!" said Leygon, "Where is it exactly?"

"Well, I've never been too good with giving directions, so how about I lead you chaps there? I was just about to grab meself a tankard of mead anyhow."

Leygon looked over at Taelor, and Taelor met eyes with Leygon before giving the man a small nod.

And so they dismounted their horses and walked them at their sides, following the man down the cobblestone path, noting many a shabby property as they went along.

"Why the biggest one, Leygon?" Taelor asked under his breath.

Leygon shrugged. "It was just what came to mind."

"The bigger the place, the larger the crowds, the more people to recognize me," Taelor said despairingly.

"Not necessarily," said Lance. "The biggest pub doesn't always draw the biggest crowds. And the way I see it, the more people there, the smaller chance you'll be noticed."

"Well, here we are, chaps!" said the man, gesturing to The Big Bull and the Hatted Hare. It was a nicer establishment than most they had passed by, and a cozy glow came from the open windows.

There was a stable around one side of the inn, and the trio left their two horses there for the night. Then, Leygon, being used to serving Taelor, purposely got to the front door first so that he could hold it open for him. Taelor walked through, and then, for the sake of jest, Leygon shut it in Lance's face.

"Thou curly-haired little weasel!" Lance exclaimed, ruffling Leygon's yellow curls.

Taelor stepped inside and looked about the common room. The place felt stuffy from the body heat of the rowdy crowd, and the smell of ale clung to the air like a newborn's hand around his mother's finger. He looked around and saw raggedy men with sweaty brows and women dressed revealingly, the room filled with the din of all their drunken laughter. Then brushing right past him, heading to the doorway, was a man yet again with the face of Naelor. Taelor jumped and once more felt the color leave his face, but the man had soon disappeared.

The trio seated themselves at a small table, and Leygon ordered two chicken legs and a baked potato, Taelor a steak cooked well and a cup of wine, and Lance his anticipated smoked ham and a tankard of ale. They ate in near silence. Once Lance had finished his meal, Taelor noticed that he gazed around the common room hopefully, then rolled his eyes.

"Well," he said to Taelor, "I was wrong about you not being noticed. And I happen to resent you."

"Most of Minear does," answered Taelor in the depressing tone he had been speaking in as of late.

"No, not because of that," said Lance, "It was stupid of you, but truth is I had little love for Naelor. Why do you think I volunteered to accompany you when your uncle asked all the knights?" Lance gave Taelor a swift nod, raising his eyebrows and pressing his lips. "The reasons I resent you are because you're no fun at all, and so moody. Not just because of… what happened, but you've always had a sort of mood about you, haven't ya? If I were you, I think I'd be the happiest man in all the lands! Every woman throws you a lustful gaze. Every. Single. Bloody. Woman. And you don't even notice! Because you're too busy with all your gloomy thoughts!"

Taelor was indifferent, looking down into his wine with a long face. "I murdered my own father, not even a fortnight past, and you would have me cheerful?"

"Cheerfulness isn't in your nature, eh?" Lance said playfully. "I don't think I've ever seen you cheerful. I'd quite like to know if you have a fun side at all, tucked deep away in there…"

Taelor gave no response.

"Oh, there we go again with the Mr. Moody Face!" Lance sang, standing. "Now, if you don't mind, I'm off to go find someone who'll be a little more charmed by me."

"Good luck," said Taelor, still looking downward, but a small smirk crossed his face.

"But before I leave!" cried Lance, "Tell me what kind of woman you like."

"What?" Taelor asked languidly.

"What do you go for in a woman? Light hair, dark hair, light complexion, dark complexion, tall, short, thin, a little on the plump side?"

"I know what you're up to, Lance," said Taelor suspiciously, "and I'm not interested."

"Oh, I took you for a man of pleasure!"

"You took me quite wrong," said Taelor, a hint of annoyance in his voice.

"Then what's all this wine you drink?" (Taelor was now on his fourth cup).

"To drown my thoughts in. But if it were a pool and not a cup, to drown myself in."

"God!" Lance exclaimed, then leaning over to look at Leygon, said, "Is he always like this?"

Leygon gave a small shrug, smiling slightly, but his interest was in awaiting his second order of chicken legs.

"Well," Lance said, "I'm off to find any woman who'll have me. Alas!" he said to Taelor, "my selection is much smaller than yours, my new friend." Then laughing to himself, he went off in a merry manner.

Leygon ate his chicken legs, and Taelor's eyes wandered the room. It was true that many of the women had their eyes on him. It made him feel uneasy. Some looked away when his eyes moved in their direction, but most would smile at him flirtatiously. He might have blushed uncomfortably at that, but he had drunk too much wine to care. Taelor was not in the mood for strange women looking his way this night, but mostly he felt that he did not deserve their attention. He didn't feel he deserved anything, and guilt suddenly overcame him.

Then a man in the image of his father caught his eye. Taelor's heart skipped a beat. He rapidly blinked and shook his head, expecting for the vision to fade away and to see a mere stranger where he thought he had sighted his father. But the man still had Naelor's face, and he was once again adorned like a king. The man turned to face Taelor and their eyes met, at which Taelor let out a cry. Leygon looked over at Taelor and saw that he was strangely pale.

Taelor made to take a swig of wine, but something about the liquid inside the cup made him jump, and he let out a cry once again. It was not wine that he saw, but blood, dense and crimson. And then the blood seemed to ooze out of the cup and drip onto the table. In a fit of panic, Taelor threw the cup down, and when the liquid spilled and spread on the wooden surface, it appeared once again as wine. With the back of his arm, Taelor wiped the cold sweat that beaded on his brow and made a hazy gesture to Leygon that he was going up to their room. He turned to leave, hardly aware that his feet were leading him upstairs.

Leygon was especially concerned about Taelor at this moment and was not prepared to let him go off on his own. He grabbed their belongings and followed after his master.

Leygon was now walking by Taelor's side, and Taelor mumbled something incoherent.

They walked down the hallway in silence and soon came to their room. Leygon opened the door for Taelor, then followed, closing it behind them.

There were two beds, one at each side of the room, each with a little wooden table next to it. Leygon knew that Taelor preferred to sleep farther away from the door, and so laid his belongings by the first bed they came to as they walked in.

It was late, so they soon put out the candles and got into bed. But Taelor was acting strange that night, even stranger than he had been acting. Wishing for his friend to sleep with an eased mind, he asked Taelor what was bothering him.

But Taelor only said, with an element of emptiness to his voice, "I love my half-sister, but I wish I had never met her. I wish she had never come to Minear. Then none of this would have happened, and my father would be alive."

Leygon felt a pang inside him, and his eyes shut as he tried to think of something to say in condolence. However, the few things that came to mind were useless, and he was better off saying nothing at all.

But after a moment he said tenderly, "Get some rest, Taelor. The new day will come bright, and when you awake, I will bring you the food of your choice."

Taelor did not respond, and Leygon wished he could have said something better to his friend. But he did not know what to say or what to do. Still, he could not just drift off in slumber, knowing how Taelor was feeling. He lay in bed, restless. And before long he could hear Taelor sobbing into his bedsheets. It started off barely audible, his irregular breathing pattern being the only indication. But then his sobs became more violent, and he would inhale sharply.

A punch in the stomach would not have caused Leygon much more pain than this. He slid out from under his sheets, walked over to Taelor, and sat at the edge of his bed. Taelor was facing the other way, and Leygon laid a hand on his back and gently said, "I'm with you, Taelor. And I always will be. I'll try to lift the darkness when I can."

Taelor's sobs began to ease. He tried to calm himself and control his breathing, and soon he was better. He turned around and sat up, his back resting against the headboard. His eyes were red and puffy, but the room was completely dark, save for a stream of moonlight coming through the window. "Leygon, truest of friends," he said, "I know I will always have thee. And for that, I am immensely grateful. Only, I do not believe I deserve such a friend."

"Nonsense, Taelor. You are the humblest prince I could ever have imagined. You always treated me with uncommon respect."

Taelor gave something of a shrug. "Prince, lord, domestic, what of it? What is high blood or low blood? Is it not of the same stuff? Think not so highly of me, Leygon, just because I have decency. What is decency when it is paired with patricide and regicide?"

After a moment, Leygon said, "Nonetheless you showed chivalry and justness. You are decent, chivalrous, and just."

"I am a murderer, traitor, and the worst son in all the kingdoms," said Taelor, facing the window. "Goodnight, Leygon. Sleep soundly and deeply. I can no longer, for my conscience prevents it. Sweet sleep belongs to the sweet. My kind is doomed to long, lonely, restless nights of self-loathing."

Tired as he was, Leygon said, "I cannot sleep knowing you can't. I will stay up with you."

"Dearest Leygon, thou wilt not, I allow it not. Sleep. I am well enough."

"What will you do all the night?"

"Stare out the window, wishing I was any man or woman I see pass by." The window was a hole in the wall the size of a head, and the cool night air was entering through it. It looked out to the street.

The hours dragged, but finally, overcome with weariness, Taelor put his head down and slept. When he awoke of his own accord, it was past midday, and Leygon brought him bread and sausages, as he had requested. As Taelor was eating, Leygon swallowed and prepared to tell his friend some news which he knew he would not take well.

"Taelor," he started.

"'Tis Tev now," Taelor corrected patiently.

"Yes, Tev… Unfortunately, something happened in the night… Something scared the horses away, and they're nowhere to be found… including Minny…"

Taelor paused his chewing, his expression blank.

"Lance borrowed a horse from somewhere else and went off early this morning to look for Minny," Leygon continued.

"What? He just went off? Did he say when he would be back?"

"Well, no… Just whenever he finds Minny and makes his way back…"

"So, are we to wait here for him, not knowing when he might return?"

"Nay," said Leygon. "He doesn't expect us to. He said he'd catch up with us. He said he's good at finding horses and even better at finding people…"

"Oh, that is well," said Taelor sarcastically, displeased.

"He knows how much Minny means to you… He must really care about you."

It had now sunk in that Minny was lost. He nodded his head to agree with Leygon.

"So, we'll set out this afternoon, without Lance?" Taelor asked.

"Yes," said Leygon. "Well, 'tis your call, of course."

Taelor gave a small nod of his head. "I want not to spend too long in one place."

Once Taelor had finished eating and had paid the house with a handful of bronze coins, he and Leygon set out.

"Now, Leygon," said Taelor as they walked, "I want thee to feel comfortable with thy sword. Do thou like the weight of it, and the feel of the hilt when thy fingers grasp it?"

"Yes, it seems a good enough sword for me."

Then Taelor looked into Leygon's face, and the purity and innocence of Leygon struck him. "I want not for thee to have to kill someone, Leygon," he said, "Thou art no killer." Then, thinking back to his first contact killing, he sighed. "I remember clearly the first man I slew with sword. It was at the Battle of the Green Field. I can still see his face. He would have struck a blow at Sir Paldir when he was at unawares, fighting another man and facing the opposite direction. But I barged through the Kingsguard and got him in the gut. I can recall in great clarity what he looked like as he lay there dying." He paused, then continued with, "I wept that night as I cleaned his blood from my sword. And my father came over and said that I cannot grieve for all those whose lives I end, that there will be many more to come."

Then with a hollowness about his voice, "If only he knew who the next man I killed with my sword would be..."

For a moment, he felt like he would weep, but he did everything in his power to prevent it. He had suffered Leygon to witness him weep enough this past week. He would not let it happen yet again.

Leygon thought he was better off saying nothing in response.

The air was still, yet there was a crisp chillness that seemed to penetrate the skin. But the miles that Taelor and Leygon walked warmed their bodies. They had been traveling for a few hours and had found themselves in a thicket of trees. Suddenly, Taelor stopped. He gestured to Leygon that he should keep still and gazed around warily. Then he slowly drew his sword and moved in close to Leygon. Frightened, Leygon followed Taelor's actions and drew his own sword. Then about ten men appeared from behind the trees, coming from all different directions and encircling them, each with an arrow set to his bow. Taelor and Leygon were trapped.

"What is the meaning of this?" said Taelor.

"We don't like outsiders in these woods," said one of the men.

"Then we will leave," replied Taelor.

"Oh, no, you won't," answered the man, and turning to the others, he said, "Grab 'em and bring 'em back to our spot. Disarm 'em and tie 'em each to a tree. I'll question 'em later."

A few men then hurried over to Taelor and Leygon, some with arrows still set to their bows, which they pointed at them threateningly. In despair, Taelor threw up his hands, and Leygon did the same. The men took away their swords and grabbed their bags. Taelor and Leygon were dragged through the trees and brought to a patch of flat land encircled with many tall oaken trunks. There were more men sitting around, watching as Taelor and Leygon were brought forth.

And as Taelor was dragged along, he saw a thin, swarthy woman who seemed to be about his age tied to one of the trees. She was scantily dressed, and a broken bow of simple craftsmanship and several snapped arrows were at her feet. She had long dark hair tied in a braid that fell over her shoulder and reached to her hip, and her eyes were fixed on one of the men who sat on the patch of ground before her. She looked at this man with such fierce detest, and her gaze did not waver, even when Taelor and Leygon were dragged right past her. There was something about this woman that attracted Taelor, more than her body or face or hair. Taelor and Leygon were tied to trees themselves. Taelor was right across from the young woman, and his eyes kept drifting over to her.

Soon the leader of the men approached Taelor and Leygon, his walk and speech revealing drunkenness.

"Now, which one should I question first?" he called out to his company, "Blondie or Pretty Boy?"

The men chortled obnoxiously, and the leader walked around the spot where Taelor and Leygon each were tied, sizing them up.

He stopped at Leygon and said, "How old are you, boy?"

"Twenty," said Leygon.

The man let out a cruel and drunken laugh. "Twenty?" he jeered, "I woulda thought you were newly come into your teen years... Well, perhaps you are, and you're just too simple to count your years, eh?"

"Leygon is sharp, unlike thy drunk self," said Taelor, "And I would rather have his lasting youthfulness than look like a sweaty old half-troll..."

A queer smirk curved the lips of the man, and he moved over to Taelor with a strange glint in his eye. "A sweaty old half-troll, eh? Well, I s'pose it's better than being prettier than a fancy gowned woman with a painted face and styled hair," he mocked Taelor, before giving him a backhanded slap.

Taelor's left cheek stung from the blow.

"Well, I guess I'll question you first," said the man, "Let's see how that sharp tongue of yours answers my questions."

"Very well," said Taelor, "Ask away."

"Where do you come from?" asked the man.

"The kingdom of Laiden."

"What brings you down 'ere?"

"Private business," said Taelor.

The man looked him up and down. "Are you a noble?"

"No," said Taelor, "But I am a knight. King Sederr sent me on a quest, which has brought me hither—though this is not my intended destination."

"I doubt that not," said the man with a wry grin. Then gesturing to Leygon, he said, "Who's your companion?"

"He's my squire."

"I see," said the man, then he turned away and sat down with the rest of the men.

"Are you satisfied?" Taelor called out, "Can we be let go now?"

The man ignored Taelor, and for an hour, Taelor and Leygon stood, tied against a tree. There was a young boy amongst the men who Taelor did not at first notice. He had reddish-brown hair, and his ears were too big for his head. The men would make him fetch wood, start fires, clean their boots, and whet their weapons. Taelor watched this boy, pitying him. At one point, the boy was washing caked mud off a pair of boots but could not manage to get them completely clean, at which the leader of the men hit him over the head and called him useless.

Taelor would not stand for this. "Useless thou call him, yet I have watched him do all the work whilst thou drink thyself drunker than a jaundiced jester."

The man chortled evilly. "Ah, the knight in shining armor 'as some nerve, don't 'e now?"

"A good leader respects his followers," said Taelor dismissively.

"Ah, well, you see," said the man, "My 'followers' are not knights like yourself. They're outlaws, and I'm their captain, not a God-appointed, high-blooded king. They have no knight's code, and I have no king's code, or whatever it is a king farts. The rules are: *I say, and they do*; and if they don't like the way I treat 'em, well that's just too bleedin' bad."

"And how do you expect to keep the loyalty of your men if you treat them like slaves? Do you fear not revolt?"

"Can't say I do," said the man, and then pointing to the boy, he said, "And this one 'ere is not a man. 'E's just an eleven-year-old boy."

"Thirteen," the boy corrected him sheepishly.

"Oh, shut up, you!" said the man, "Eleven, thirteen, what's the difference? Point is you're not a man."

"Yet still he is more of a man than you," said Taelor.

At this, the man arose and approached Taelor once again. He stared at him a while, then threw a punch at his mouth. "I've 'eard quite enough from you," he said. "Keep that pretty little mouth of yours shut."

The punch was not too hard, for which Taelor was grateful.

Time passed once again, every moment of being tied to the tree feeling longer than it really was. Then eventually, one of the men amongst the outlaws, who appeared to be even drunker than the captain, approached the woman who stood tied to the tree opposite Taelor. The man looked upon her with lust and reached out his hands to her chest.

"Don't touch her," Taelor said boldly and disgustedly.

The man turned around to face Taelor, a vulgar grin plastered on his face. "Bugger off," he said, "Turn your 'ead if you don't want to watch."

"Don't touch her," Taelor repeated sternly. Then after a moment's thought, he continued, "'Tis for your own good. You don't want to touch her. She is of the wild folk. Her people carry disease. I have watched men die in agony who have come in physical contact with her kind."

The trick worked. The man gave the woman a quick glance, his countenance wary and fearful, then turned and walked back to where the other men sat.

Taelor had but a moment to feel satisfied. The captain of the outlaws overheard what he had said, and blurted, "That's another lie!"

Taelor was startled. "*Another lie?*"

"Aye," said the captain, stepping onto his feet and approaching Taelor once again, unable to hide how much he was enjoying himself. "The first was that you're a knight. I asked if you were a noble and you said no, but then you said you're a knight: a Laiden knight of King Sederr. And there you revealed to me two things: one, that you're not a knight at all, because Sederr only knights those of noble blood, and two, that you're obviously not from Laiden if you don't know that. So now I don't know what to believe! All I know is you're a liar! And then you lied just now by saying the wild folk carry disease. Oh, believe me, boy, I've touched enough wild women to know that ain't true!"

Taelor felt stupid. *King Sederr only knights those of noble blood*; he knew this.

"Shoot 'im already!" one of the men yelled.

Others then joined. "Shoot 'im, shoot 'im!" they chanted.

Leygon yelled, "NO! Please, no! He won't talk out anymore, I promise!"

The captain did not respond to Leygon but just grinned his evil, drunken grin and went off to fetch his bow. Then strolling toward Taelor, he stopped within around fifteen feet of him.

Putting an arrow to the string, he said, "Now, I'll try to make it a quick death, boy, but I can't make any guarantees. I'm quite drunk, like as you put it, drunker than a jaundiced jester. And jesters aren't known for their good aim, now are they?"

The men chortled and cheered, looking on with hungry eyes. Leygon, hollering, tried desperately to break free. Taelor could hardly sense anything. The world had become hazy, and only vague shapes could be made out, not figures nor trees. All he could feel was his heart banging around in his chest like a desperate animal trying to free itself from a cage.

But just as the captain pulled back the arrow and got ready to release, the thirteen-year-old boy, who was in the middle of sharpening a knife, barged through the men and before anyone could stop him, jammed the knife into the captain's back. A ghastly croak came from the captain, and he collapsed onto the ground with his bow, his arrow springing away feebly and landing near his dead body.

In utter shock, the men glanced between the boy and their dead captain. Taelor, who was looking away, turning his head so as not to see the arrow when it came for him, turned back around and stared at the scene unbelieving. His life had been saved! He was saved by the boy he had stood up for. He had never appreciated his life so much than at this moment.

Immense relief washed over him. He looked at the boy in wonder, and love for him welled in his heart. In that moment, he made up his mind to befriend the boy, bring him along with himself and Leygon, and to protect him and care for him as an older brother would. After all, he owed him his life.

But then Taelor saw the scene turn for the worse. Anger appeared on the faces of the men, and they took up their bows and pointed at the boy to avenge their captain, whilst others pointed at Taelor. But as soon as panic once again consumed Taelor, a great gust of wind came to blow down the outlaws, knocking them off their feet and preventing them from getting back up.

Also at that moment, the sky became a nightmarish gray, and a dark phantom the size of ten trees came swiftly gliding right in the direction of the outlaws, letting out a breathless, deathlike groan as it came. The men belted screams that conveyed such potent terror, screams that came right from the gut and scratched the throat, almost loud enough to burst eardrums. They dropped their bows and arrows where they stood and ran off into the woods like ants scattering.

The boy, who had been standing with his arms over his face, looked ahead of him with wide eyes, watching as the men ran off, screaming their throats out, the phantom chasing after them. Then when the men were far, running ever farther from Taelor, Leygon, the boy, and the woman, the phantom turned back toward the captives. No longer, however, was it gliding swiftly, but now just floated, almost bobbing, over to where the four were. Then it changed form and no longer looked like an evil mass of black smoke. It morphed into a more precise figure, and Taelor watched incredulous, tears welling in his eyes. The phantom was now in the image of King Naelor. It came slowly and gently up to Taelor and looked upon him lovingly, and Taelor, who opened his mouth to speak (in vain, for he could utter no word), stared into the face of his father and saw that it was young and that years of care had somehow been lifted from it. He seemed at peace, happy, and almost relieved. He must have now been in the world of the dead, reunited with Taelor's mother. Tears fell from Taelor's face. But before he could wonder any further, the ghost vanished in an instant.

Taelor, Leygon, the boy, and the woman stood in awe at what they just beheld. The woman beckoned the boy to cut her bonds and free her from the tree. He did so, and then he cut the ropes that restrained Taelor and Leygon. They all looked at each other, feeling a sense of companionship.

Leygon concluded that he should be the one to break the silence, for both Taelor and the boy were especially shaken by what had taken place, and he was not sure whether the woman could even speak the same tongue as they.

Looking into both the boy and woman's faces, he said, "I am called Leygon. What are your names?"

"Rendy," said the boy, his voice hoarse and shaky.

"Ukanzah," said the woman.

"'Tis lovely to meet you both," said Leygon, then gesturing to Taelor, he said, "This is my companion and good friend, Tael—" then remembering what Taelor now wished to be called, he corrected himself, saying, "Tev."

Rendy gazed up at Taelor with big eyes. He could not remember the last time someone cared about him enough to stick up for him. Ukanzah looked upon Taelor before turning and reaching down to pick up a bow that one of the men had let fall and then gathered a supply of arrows from the ground.

"They break mine," she said angrily, spitting on the ground. "They kill my tribe, and I will get them. With arrow, that filth. If I see them, they must run fast."

Taelor took a liking to her. Facing Rendy, he looked into his freckled face and said, "I cannot express enough gratitude toward thee for saving my life. Thou art a very brave young man. Thou art under my protection now, and I will do whatever it takes to keep thee safe."

Rendy smiled a genuine smile. "Thanks, sir!" he said, "And thanks for sticking up for me before as well!"

Taelor put a hand on Rendy's shoulder. "Thou may call me Tev."

Walking over to where the outlaws had placed his and Leygon's swords and bags, Taelor brought them over. Then he led forth his companions, guiding them in the opposite direction to where most of the outlaws had fled. Eventually, when the sky was pitch dark, they found a comfortable patch of ground, with the shelter of trees, to sleep. Taelor took the first watch of the night whilst the others slept, then after a few hours, he awoke Leygon to take over whilst he got some rest himself.

Chapter 6: The Witches and the Prophecy

Taelor awoke to the sound of ruffling beside him, feeling the sting of an unrestful sleep as he opened his eyes. He turned his head in the direction of the sound and saw the boy Rendy sitting himself up. Becoming aware of the hard ground digging into his side, Taelor wondered how he had fallen asleep at all, a light, uneasy sleep though it had been. He lifted himself from the ground, and the events of the previous night came flashing through his mind. He had almost died. He couldn't suppress thoughts that told him he should have. Taelor felt he deserved to; he was probably supposed to. But how was Rendy to have known that? And he was saved, after all, not only by Rendy but also by his father's spirit. Yet what did that mean? Did his father forgive him? Did his father really still love him? Taelor's throat grew tight, and his eyes burned with tears he strove to hold back—in vain, for they welled in his eyes, blurring his vision. He hastily blinked them away.

Leygon, who was sitting a little way before them with his back to Taelor and Rendy, keeping watch, turned around at the sound of his companions' moving bodies.

"Good morning to you both!" he said with his usual bright smile.

"Mornin', Leygon!" said Rendy. Then turning to Taelor, "Mornin', Tev! Sorry if I woke you."

Taelor grunted and attempted a smile, and with an awkward gesture of his hand, he tried to tell Rendy it was all right.

Leygon grinned at Rendy. "He is oftentimes a mute at morning. Give him some time to wake up."

Taelor, seeming as one in a daze, began to look around with a puzzled expression.

Upon noticing this, Leygon said, "Oh, are you wondering about—uh, Kanzukah? She went hunting. She'll be back with our breakfast."

"Hunting," Taelor repeated dully.

"Yeah," said Leygon. "Are you not hungry? I surely am."

"Me too," said Rendy.

Taelor came to his feet and walked over to his bag. Opening it, he pulled out his crossbow and a store of arrows.

"Which direction did she take?" Taelor asked in a groggy voice.

"She went that way," replied Leygon, pointing west.

Taelor went off to find her, crossbow at his side.

As he disappeared into the trees, Taelor faintly heard the voice of Rendy saying, "I'll collect supplies for a fire, Leygon," and soon enough, hurried footsteps sounded from behind. He turned and saw Rendy approaching, a small smile on his freckled face.

"Hello, Rendy," Taelor greeted.

"I've never been 'untin' before, Tev. Neither 'ave I used a crossbow. Actually, I ain't ever used any weapon beside that knife I jammed into Kadef's back last night."

"And I am eternally in thy debt for doing so. I shall teach thee how to shoot from crossbow one day. I will train thee in swordsmanship as well."

"Will you really?" Rendy asked brightly.

"I will," Taelor confirmed with a small nod of his head.

"Well, I'm off to grab some shredded bark, dry grass, or whatever I can find 'ere. And some twigs and logs, for a fire."

Taelor nodded appreciatively. And with that, the boy turned and went off.

Taelor walked on, scanning the area, trying to catch sight of Ukanzah. The morning came with fog, making the task a difficult one. As he was wondering how far she had gotten, and whether he was even heading in her direction, a great weariness suddenly consumed him, and he stumbled. He fell onto his knees, and the forest seemed to swim about him. He kneeled thus, hands on the ground for support, waiting for the sensation to cease.

It came to be that Ukanzah found him this way. Hands full with two slain rabbits, she looked upon him. But Taelor seemed unaware, his head hung, and his thick hair obscuring his face. Ukanzah stepped closer. Finally, Taelor sensed a presence, and lifting his head as one fearful, he gazed up at Ukanzah. Humiliation dominated all other feelings, and he got back onto his feet, standing tall and straight.

"Ukanzah," he greeted.

"You not feel good?" she asked.

"I'm all right now," he answered.

Ukanzah rested the two rabbits on one arm, and with the other, stretched out her hand, resting her palm on Taelor's forehead, feeling for a temperature.

"You not hot," she stated. "Come."

Taelor grabbed the rabbits from Ukanzah's arms and carried them for her, which she seemed to neither expect nor appreciate. The two walked back to where they had left Leygon and Rendy, neither speaking a word. Once they had reached the spot, Rendy was kindling a small flame, and Leygon watched, eyes wide and mouth agape as the boy fed the growing fire.

"I've never seen someone start a fire so quickly," Leygon spoke to Taelor and Ukanzah as they approached.

"Well done, Rendy," said Taelor, to which the boy smiled. He had never felt appreciated amongst the outlaws, and his work was certainly never praised.

"You skin rabbits?" Ukanzah asked of Taelor whilst pulling out a small, sharp knife.

Taelor had never done so, yet not wanting to seem incompetent, he did not speak the truth. Resting the slain rabbits on his left arm and drawing his sword with his right, he realized how foolish he was for bringing only that and a crossbow for weaponry. He had not considered a small knife for skinning animals for cooking.

Ukanzah looked at him unimpressed. "I knew from right away you not good with living. You and light hair boy. You high born?"

Taelor, less offended than he thought he should have been at these words, simply said, "I am a lord. I grew up in a castle. Leygon lived in the castle chambers as well."

Ukanzah gave something of an understanding nod, took the slain rabbits from him, and said, "I do it." As she worked on skinning the first rabbit, suddenly she said to Taelor, "You think my people disease?"

Taelor was at first dumbfounded, but then remembering the excuse he had given for the outlaw not to violate her, he answered, "No! I said so to save you from being dishonored." Then assuming the word was not in Ukanzah's vocabulary, he clarified, "Touched."

Ukanzah only shot him a look, again showing no appreciation.

"Ukanzah, Rendy, do either of you have a knife I could use?" Taelor asked.

Ukanzah pulled out another small knife and handed it to Taelor. Unhappy about the job, he began skinning the other rabbit.

"I am sorry about what happened to your people," Taelor said to Ukanzah as he was working on the rabbit. "If we see that outlaw scum again, you and I will avenge your fallen together."

"We kill them," Ukanzah said, "Arrows in eyes, throats, hearts."

"Yes," Taelor consented.

"Is it the four of us now?" Leygon asked pleasantly.

"Rendy is under my protection," said Taelor, glancing over at the boy, who gazed back at him. "As for Ukanzah, she can speak for herself. What say you, Ukanzah?"

"My tribe dead or gone far," she stated simply.

"Then with us, you shall stay," Taelor answered, "so long as your heart desires it."

Ukanzah gave a small smile, if it could be called a smile.

"Rendy," Taelor said, "have you no family?"

"No," the boy answered, "my parents died when I was little. I can't remember them. And I don't 'ave a brother or sister. Not that I know of."

"I, too, no longer have parents," said Taelor.

Once the four had cooked the rabbits over the fire and eaten a substantial enough meal, following Taelor, they continued to head southeast.

Rendy walked close to Taelor. "Did you know your parents, Tev?"

"My mother died when I was very young. But I knew my father well."

"What was 'e like?"

Taelor wished Rendy would not have asked. "He was… proud. And stubborn. But he was my father nonetheless."

Rendy looked into Taelor's face, but Taelor would not meet his gaze.

"Do you 'ave a brother or sister?"

"A sister," Taelor responded.

"What's she like?"

"She's perhaps the most remarkable person I've ever known," said Taelor, then in a soft, melancholy voice, "But I may not ever see her again."

"Why's that?"

"Because Rendy," Taelor spoke, this time looking at the boy, "I had to leave my home. And I can't go back."

Rendy did not answer right away, and Taelor thought his tone must have conveyed that he did not wish to speak of it further. But then, as if the boy could restrain himself no longer, he blurted, "So you've been exiled?"

Taelor sighed. "Yes. Of sorts."

"It's all right, Tev. I 'ear people get exiled from Laiden all the time. For silly reasons, 'coz Sederr is mad."

"Mad?" Taelor said, "Well, I'm not sure I would use the same word. Though, harsh, yes. Unreasonable, stubborn. Many of the same characteristics as my late father."

"Was your father a powerful man in Laiden?"

"He was a lord."

"A big lord?"

"Yes, a big lord."

Rendy was satisfied and asked nothing further. He took out his water skin and drank heavily from it.

"Look," said Leygon, pointing in the distance. Through the thick fog, four figures in dingy robes could be distinguished, standing around something, hunched over as if they were occupied in some activity.

"What are they?" asked Taelor.

"Let's find out!" said Rendy, heading toward the figures at quite a speed.

"Rendy!" cried Taelor hurrying after him.

The figures suddenly turned their heads in the direction of the group, Taelor's cry having made their presence known. Taelor halted, wide-eyed, as did Rendy. The faces of the figures could not be seen clearly in the fog, but they each appeared incredibly old, and disproportionate, with long chins, noses, and foreheads.

"Come closer, if thou be not afraid!" called out one of them.

"We are only four women. Four very, very old women," called out another.

"Very friendly, too!" said the third.

"Reveal thyselves already, we have not all day!" demanded the fourth.

Taelor and Rendy warily approached the women, Leygon and Ukanzah lagging behind. The four old, scraggly women were huddled over a cauldron.

"O! O! Look what we've got!" exclaimed the first witch.

"They do look nice!" exclaimed the second.

"They look perfect! He, he, he, he!" exclaimed the third.

"Calm thyselves, thou blabbering old fools!" cried the fourth.

These comments unnerved Rendy. "You… You want to eat us?"

The four witches let out shrill cackles. "Eat thee?!"

"No, we only want to drink thy blood!" laughed one witch.

The other three hit her over the head. "Thou jabbering crone! Do not scare off our company!"

Then the skinniest of the witches, whose eyes were fixed on Taelor's face as soon as he came within sight, blurted, "Of drinking thou speak, and this one I know, for he once drank my tea!" She cackled. "Oh yes, my tea he drank, he did! Lo! This is Prince Taelor!"

"You!" cried Taelor heatedly.

"Prince Taelor," repeated Rendy, incredulous, looking upon Taelor in a new light. "You killed your father to take the throne, but 'e 'ad a bastard daughter who got it instead!"

Taelor, angry and stung, indignantly denied this statement. "Nay, not the reason! I never wanted the throne! I killed him because he tried to assassinate my half-sister. And I'm not proud of it! My guilt shall consume me piece by piece."

"Piece by piece," mechanically repeated a witch.

"Nay, only one piece!" cried another.

"Yes, just one piece," confirmed the Tea Witch.

"Sacrifice thy right hand, thy bloody hand, and thou shalt be relieved of thy guilt and grief forever."

"No, Taelor," cried Leygon. "Sell not into witchcraft."

"My soul is already damned," answered Taelor. "What would some witchcraft hinder? I am already stained, already doomed…"

"Taelor, you need your hand," insisted Leygon. "*We* need your hand! Your swordsmanship is the only we can trust."

"Give up thy right hand, thy bloody hand, and be free!" the witches sang in one voice.

"At what price?" demanded Taelor.

"The price of thy hand, obviously," mocked a witch.

"But will there be any other consequence?" Taelor asked.

"Nay, no other," said the first witch.

"No other," repeated the second.

"So be it," Taelor decided, "Take my hand."

He held out his right hand to the witches, and the longest-nosed amongst them brandished a large, well-whetted dagger.

"Taelor, no!" cried Leygon.

Taelor withdrew his hand. "I've changed my mind."

"But 'tis already settled," said the witch with the dagger, gesturing for Taelor's hand with her long, pale, almost dead-looking fingers.

"The sacrifice must be carried through," agreed another.

"Fear not," said the Tea Witch. "Thou wilt bleed not."

"Thou wilt feel no pain," said the witch with the dagger, nearing Taelor. "Cometh, thou fallen prince, to the cauldron. Hold thy hand over!"

An outside force compelled Taelor to forfeit his right hand to the witches. The dagger-wielding witch grabbed hold of Taelor's arm with her brisk grip, elevating the dagger, ready to plunge it down upon Taelor's wrist. Taelor winced, turning his head away. Next, he heard horror-filled gasps from his friends behind, and, molesting his eardrums, the cackles of the witches. He turned his head back around and looked at his wrist. It was now a stub. But incredibly, he felt not a thing, and no blood issued from his crippled arm. But in the cauldron, he saw his hand, a ghastly white hand with spidery fingers, swimming in a pool of dense red. His head became light, his vision blurring, stomach turning. He collapsed onto the ground.

The voices of the witches swam through Taelor's semiconscious mind. They spoke the words, "King of Minear thou wilt yet become, but like thy father, thou wilt be slain by the hand of thy son." And again, *"King of Minear thou wilt yet become, but like thy father, thou wilt be slain by the hand of thy son."* The witches cackled ferociously, and yet repeated, *"KING OF MINEAR THOU WILT YET BECOME, BUT LIKE THY FATHER, THOU WILT BE SLAIN BY THE HAND OF THY SON."*

Taelor awoke, breathing heavily, clammy-faced, crazy-eyed. "What tall tale was that?!" he shouted to the witches who were hovering about him. "I have no son!"

"We give no explanations," said one.

"We only tell," said another.

"What son?" Taelor pleaded. "I have no son unless you breed one from that ghastly hand!"

The witches only cackled.

"What will you do with the hand?" Taelor cried, "What in God's name have I unleashed?"

"Worry not, Taelor," said the Tea Witch, "'Tis only our supper."

The witches laughed, "He, he, he, he!"

"Get thyselves back to Hell!" thundered Taelor.

And with that, the witches, still cackling, joined hands around the cauldron, and in an instant, disappeared themselves from the physical world.

Leygon, Rendy, and Ukanzah were each turned to stone in their horror. Finally, Leygon, swinging his head around to Taelor, exclaimed, "Why?"

Taelor, forlorn, did not answer for a moment. But then he spoke, "We must go back to Minear. I fear for Alene's safety."

Chapter 7: The Vengeance and the Returning Friend

Taelor did not want to look at the stub on the end of his arm, and his companions didn't have many words, not even Rendy. But they all wanted to get out of that forest. It was nothing but an endless, ominous trap of trees and fog and darkness. They couldn't even remember from which direction they came, nor could they tell which direction they were headed.

But, after some hours of mindless wandering, they heard voices and moving bodies, and sighted, but a few yards ahead, a group of some twenty to thirty men, amidst the trees. The men did not notice Taelor and his company. Taelor quietly bent down, the others following his action, and crawled, or slithered, toward the men. Ukanzah was the first to recognize them. She made something of a hissing sound upon her recognition. Taelor signaled to her to wait. He was evaluating the scene and trying to figure the best way to strike. But Ukanzah couldn't have seen his signal, for she already had a bow to her arrow, and in an instant, she aimed and shot one of the men in the side of his neck. Right as Taelor saw this happen, he turned his head around to look at Ukanzah. Only half a second could have passed before she already had another arrow to her bow and shot again, her arrow this time landing in a man's back, piercing his heart. Her face was hard and cold, her eyes sharp and ready. Most of the outlaws had let their bows fall when they were scurrying away from the ghastly phantom of Naelor, so they were defenseless—like much of Ukanzah's tribe when the outlaws came and massacred them.

Ukanzah shot again and again and again, never missing. Taelor had only just drawn his crossbow. But struggling with just a stub at the end of his right arm, he had barely put an arrow in the device before, looking up, he saw that half the men were dead, and Ukanzah, having run out of arrows, began to reach into his bag to take his store, and continued shooting at the outlaws again. But an arrow coming from one of the outlaws stuck her in the side, and she fell.

"No!" Taelor yelled as he got onto his feet and drew the knife Ukanzah had given him. He ran full force at the outlaw with the bow, but in the next instant, an arrow pierced the man. Taelor looked back around at Ukanzah, but she was still lying on the ground. Then looking out ahead, Taelor saw the figure of a horse and rider ripping through the fog, a bow in the rider's hand. He recognized them quickly. It was Lance and Minny! There were two outlaws still standing, neither armed with a bow. Lance, riding in their direction, grabbed them each by the collars of their shirts and dragged them along, bringing them to Taelor.

"These fellas causing you trouble, are they?" asked Lance.

Taelor was so relieved and gladdened at his friend's reappearance, that in his brief moment of glee he had forgotten that Ukanzah was badly injured. Upon remembering, he lifted the knife he had clenched in his left hand, and the two men, pitiful in Lance's hold, had but seconds to beg for their lives before Taelor made a gash in each of their throats.

"Not anymore they aren't," Taelor answered, watching the men as they choked and gagged and coughed up blood before falling lifeless.

Lance looked upon Taelor simultaneously shocked and impressed. "Well, I must say… that was unexpected coming from you."

Taelor met Lance's gaze, his expression dark. "I am glad you're back, Lance," he said, then he went to embrace his beloved horse and said, "And thee, Minny." The horse nuzzled into Taelor's shoulder.

Looking down at Taelor's arms around Minny, Lance let out a yelp. He jumped down from the horse, ripped Taelor's right arm away, and looking at the stub, exclaimed, "What in God's name happened?"

"Long story," Taelor sighed. "I'll tell you later."

"How in the world did it heal so quickly? The skin over it! Taelor, or Tev, whatever your bleedin' name is, what the bloody hell could—how—what—how did this happen?"

"Witches," Taelor said.

"Witches? Good God, Taelor, I leave you for little more than a day, and you go lose your swordhand to witches?"

Taelor ignored him. "My new companion and friend, Ukanzah, has an arrow in her side, and I can't ride like I used to," he said, acknowledging his stub. "Take her and get her aid. Make sure she lives."

Taelor and Lance then went over to Ukanzah together. Leygon and Rendy were looking over her, and Taelor heard Rendy ask Leygon if he should pull the arrow out, his hand reaching to it. "No!" Leygon said, hitting the boy's hand away.

"That is right," Taelor said, and putting his hand on Rendy's head to come across less harsh, he said to the boy, "Ukanzah could bleed to death if you were to do that."

Lance briefly greeted Leygon and introduced himself to Rendy. Taelor went to pick Ukanzah up by lifting her at her arms and upper body, and Lance by her calves. Lance mounted Minny, and together Lance and Taelor worked on laying Ukanzah in front of Lance. She moaned weakly.

"I'll go back to Gitbury and find a surgeon," said Lance. "Then I'll give someone your descriptions and tell them to look out for you and guide you to us. I'll pay them, of course... And oh!" he said, reaching into his pocket and pulling out something, "You'll be needing this more than I do, I think." He placed a compass in Taelor's hand.

Taelor nodded appreciatively. "Thank you, Lance. I know not what we'd do without you."

Lance grinned. "To tell you the truth, neither do I!" He laughed. "You'll want to be heading west," he informed, then he looked down at Ukanzah and back at Taelor. "Maybe once she's better, I can see you smile for once in your life, eh?" Then he turned the horse and rode off, seeming sure in his sense of direction.

Taelor looked at Leygon and Rendy. "Too bad the outlaws didn't have horses," he said. Then curiously, he asked, "Rendy, can thou ride?"

"Not really," said Rendy.

"Then I guess we're not missing out," said Taelor.

"'Tis a very good thing your uncle sent Lance off with us," Leygon said to Taelor.

Taelor made a gesture which conveyed how strongly he agreed with Leygon's comment. "A very good thing, indeed."

Chapter 8: The Training, the Recovery, and Pascale

Taelor, Leygon, and Rendy eventually made it to the edge of the forest, and but a ways ahead in the distance, they saw the signs of civilization. Once they entered the city of Gitbury, they were soon enough spotted by a man who recognized them promptly. He was a tall young man who seemed amused by the task given to him by Lance.

Upon seeing Taelor, he chuckled. "You must be Tev," he said. "You really are prettier than I'd ever fantasize my wife, and you *do* have the face of a mopey old donkey."

Taelor rolled his eyes. "All right. Where are Lance and Ukanzah?"

"Right over here," said the young man, "Just follow me." He led the way. "You three really are very distinctive looking fellows. Made my job rather simple."

The young man led them to a large surgeon house nearing the center of town, walked inside with them to collect his money from Lance, and found him napping on an old beige couch in the front room.

A woman's voice sounded from behind. "Who's hurt?" she asked the four who just entered.

"No one," answered Taelor, turning to see an aging, plump little woman behind a small wooden desk. "We're here for our friend Ukanzah. She must have been brought here around an hour past. She suffered an arrow to the side."

The woman looked rather confused. "I don't recall an Ukanzah," she said. "But we do have one Kunzana who was brought to us just before, and she suffered the same injury as you described your friend did."

"I think she must be the one," Taelor answered shortly.

Rendy made his way over to Lance napping on the couch and slapped him hard around the face. "Wake up, we're 'ere now!" he said as Lance's eyes widened, and startled, he sat up.

"Oh good God," Lance exclaimed, rubbing his face where Rendy had slapped him. Then looking at the company, he said, "Glad you made it!"

"Where's Ukanzah?" Taelor asked, gazing between the woman and Lance.

"She's getting stitched up, down the corridor, in the hall of flesh wounds," said the woman. "But the surgeons don't let anyone enter when they're doing their work."

"When will I be able to see her?" Taelor asked.

"On the morrow, when they move her to the recovery room."

"Then I shall return on the morrow."

He saw Lance in the corner paying the young man with a few small copper coins, saying, "I do hope you didn't tell them the descriptions I gave." Taelor noted that Lance had a smirk on his face.

"He told me mine," Taelor said. Then annoyed, he added, "And I'm *not pretty.*"

"Oh, you're not, are you?" Lance jested. "Then my hair's not brown!"

Taelor was unamused.

"And there," Lance started, pointing at Taelor's face, "is the mopey old donkey!"

Both Lance and the young man laughed heartily at Taelor's expense.

"I'm really not in the mood," said Taelor. He looked down at the stub at the end of his arm. It felt so strange to no longer have his right hand. He still felt like he could grab and hold with it, clench his fist, and move his fingers, but there was nothing there. He looked upon his stub pitifully. It was foul to behold. He was a cripple. He would have to get used to performing every task with only his left hand now, and most importantly, learn to fight again, wielding his sword in his less dominant hand. He wondered how he could have been so stupid.

"Lance," he said suddenly, "you'll be training me in swordsmanship. I need to become skillful with my left hand."

"You do, don't you," agreed Lance, heading over and clapping a hand around Taelor's shoulder. "I'll get you good, don't you worry."

"But as for now," Taelor said, "let's find us each a comfortable bed. I'm exhausted, and it seems you are, too."

"You read my heart's very desire," Lance chuckled. "There's an inn just a small ways down the road. This town's full of them."

"Leygon, Rendy, are either of thou in want of sleep?" Taelor asked.

"'Tis only afternoon," said Leygon.

"I'd rather a beer," said Rendy.

Lance chortled.

"Get Leygon to have one, too," Taelor said to Rendy. "Maybe thou can teach him to have a good time. God knows I haven't been much fun." Taelor smiled at Leygon.

"Not just one," said Lance, grinning between Rendy and Leygon, "Get him to have a few! He's been serving Tev, and we know that's got to be thirsty work!" Lance slapped Taelor's back whilst he said it.

"All right," Leygon said awkwardly.

"A couple of tankards, for me," Taelor winked.

Leygon grinned at that.

Taelor and Lance left Leygon and Rendy and headed for the inn. The weather had really warmed up, and they felt the sun beam upon their backs. The inn was called The Tiger's Tail. Once they got themselves situated, they went up to their room which contained two single beds.

Gesturing to Lance's, Taelor said, "I'm sorry 'tis only big enough for one."

"Why, so you can't keep me warm through the night?" Lance joked as he got into bed and pulled the covers over himself.

"Not me," Taelor chuckled as he, too, got into bed. "A woman. I realize you must be disappointed."

"Ah, not tonight," Lance said sleepily. "I was up all of last night searching for your bleedin' horse."

"I can't express my gratitude enough, Lance. Thank you for finding Minny. Where did you leave him?"

"In some stables 'round the corner," Lance answered groggily. "He better not run off again. I won't be the one hunting for him next time."

Taelor paused thoughtfully. "Maybe it was my father's phantom that frightened the horses away…"

"What was that?" mumbled Lance.

The next thing Taelor heard was Lance snoring. He rolled over and tried to fall asleep amidst the loud, rumbling sound. And the next thing he heard after that was Lance's voice in his ear, saying, "Wakey, wakey, Sleeping Beauty!" Lance's breath was warm against the side of Taelor's face. Taelor forced his eyes open and sat up. "'Tis past midday, you lazy bones!"

"That late?" Taelor asked.

"Aye, that late. And we've got a busy day of training ahead!"

Leygon came into the room, a plate of fried eggs and spinach in his hands. Lance sat across the room on his bed and drew a couple of blunt swords. Leygon served the plate to Taelor and handed him a fork.

"Thank you, Leygon," said Taelor, his left hand cutting awkwardly at the egg whites.

Lance lifted the two blunt swords and showed them to Taelor. They were borrowed swords, one longer and narrower, the other shorter and wider. "Which one do you like?"

"The long one," Taelor said.

"To match your long face," Lance teased.

Taelor rolled his eyes. "Where's Rendy?" he asked his two friends.

"Playing with some girls," said Leygon. "He's made friends with twin girls around his age."

"Twins?" Lance smirked with raised eyebrows. "Lucky lad!"

"They've been play-fighting and hiding and chasing after each other all day," said Leygon.

And sure enough, when Taelor had finished his breakfast and left the inn with Lance and Leygon, he spotted Rendy and the two girls running around the courtyard outside. The twins were a head shorter than Rendy, two scraggly girls with brown hair as messy as their clothes. Taelor thought at one point that he had caught Rendy's eye and he gave him an awkward wave with his good arm, but Rendy seemed not to notice.

Taelor insisted on visiting Ukanzah before he and Lance began their training. The three entered the recovery room and found Ukanzah lying in one of the beds. She was sleeping, but her eyes opened when she felt the presence of Taelor approaching. Her eyes found his face as he looked softly into hers and spoke her name. Only half-realizing what he was doing, his lips moved toward her brow and kissed her forehead. Looking back at Leygon and Lance, he felt his cheeks become hot. He gave Ukanzah's hand that lay over her blanket a gentle tap, then turned and made to head out. Leygon mumbled a goodbye to Ukanzah as they left her.

"Not the kind of woman I pictured you with, I'll admit," Lance said as they headed for the door.

Taelor's cheeks felt hot again. "Is she not?"

"Nay," Lance snickered. "I pictured you more with a woman who'd die of happiness if you ever wrote her a poem. She's more… rough and ready. I thought you'd be with a girl who blushes and swoons. But I guess *you're* the one who blushes and swoons." Lance laughed as he slapped Taelor's back.

"I should have sent you away along with Gavin, when I had the chance," Taelor joked.

"Ah," Lance pondered, "that would have been a grave mistake."

Around the back of the surgeon house was a field of short grass. Here, Lance trained Taelor whilst Leygon sat in the green and watched. Taelor's footwork was notably seasoned but having to reverse all his moves made him awkward, and his left arm was clumsy and weak. The swordplay continued for hours, and by the end, Taelor was getting good. He could hold his own against Lance. A satisfied grin spread across his face when he stuck his sword in the ground and leaned on it, catching his breath, and calling it a day.

Lance came over to him and in a raspy voice said, "You have a handsome smile. Don't deprive the world of it."

Taelor chuckled. "Thanks, Lance."

"I mean it," said Lance, "Bleedin' dimples and everything... Well, you were good! But this old man is tired and in need of ale..."

Leygon had laid himself on the grass some time ago and fallen asleep. Taelor went over and gently shook him awake by the shoulder. This felt strange because Leygon had awoken him hundreds of times, but he had never awoken Leygon before. Leygon's eyes opened wide, and he got himself up, asking Taelor how the training went.

"Lance is a very good trainer," said Taelor. "I got good toward the end."

"He did," Lance said to Leygon in agreement. "Rendy's probably already drinking at The Tiger's Tail, smart lad. Let's join him, shall we?"

Lance was right: Rendy was already drinking at The Tiger's Tail. The twin girls were no longer with him, but he had befriended a crowd of rowdy men. Taelor joined Rendy and the men. He had decided he no longer cared if he were recognized. But these men certainly didn't seem to recognize him, anyway. Lance soon came and sat with them, a jug of brown ale in hand, and Leygon with a jug of water. They had put an order in for stew. Lance poured himself and Taelor some ale.

"So, how about those twins?" Lance asked Rendy with a raise of his eyebrows.

"They left," said Rendy sadly.

"Oh, too bad," said Lance. "Thou were having a grand old time with them."

"Yeah," said Rendy. "Where are we 'eading next?"

"The castle of Minear," said Taelor. "Once Ukanzah is well enough."

A man amongst them with prominent features and a big red beard said, "I've heard it's the pits right now with the trouble they've had, that spoilt brat of a prince murdering his own father for the throne and some bastard girl getting it instead…"

The false rumor of Taelor's purpose only riled Taelor for a moment, unfair as it was. Once the man had called Alene "some bastard girl," he no longer cared about the previous words that came out of his mouth. Collected and composed, he said, "That bastard girl is the queen of Minear, and you shall refer to her as such."

"You're a noble, aren't you?" the man said, "I can always tell… You think we should all kiss the ground you walk on, treat you like you're gods on earth, work our asses off for you so you can look pretty and live your pretty little carefree lives. And that's still not enough for you, is it? You tire of all your feasts and festivities, always looking for power, even if it means killing your family, and we common folk are here slaving away, struggling to put bread on the table for *our* families…"

Lance stood, a hand on the hilt of his blunt, borrowed sword. "That's quite enough," he said, his voice still pleasant.

"What are you, his bodyguard?" mocked the man in his gravelly voice.

"Aye, I am," said Lance.

The man scoffed, taking a large swig from his tankard. "I'd piss on the whole lot of you!" he spat, and looking firmly into Taelor's face, he said, "That bastard whore on the throne most of all!"

Anger seethed through Taelor's body like lava through an erupting volcano. Jolting up, he got a hold of the clay jug of water by the lip using his left hand, and although awkwardly, in an instant he managed to smash it down upon the man's head. It broke asunder, knocking the man unconscious. He fell from his seat down onto the floor, blood pouring forth from his scalp. Taelor felt the arms of Lance around him, protecting him and moving him along. Leygon followed, shaken, and Rendy behind, looking back on the scene. A large crowd quickly accumulated around the unconscious man.

Lance was leading Taelor across the common room, heading for the stairs that led up to their room. A suave, dark man in all black clothing came into Taelor's vision, his gaze set on Taelor, a glint in his eyes and a smirk on his face. Once he was within a couple of feet from Taelor, he said, "That was nice," as he passed him. His accent was foreign.

Taelor turned to look back at this strange man. The man still had his eyes on him. He winked at Taelor. Slightly unsettled, Taelor turned his head.

"Who was that man?" he asked out loud.

"Don't ask me," said Lance.

The next evening, Taelor met this strange man again. Taelor had visited Ukanzah and trained with Lance again that day, and to his delight, both Ukanzah and his swordsmanship were getting stronger. When the sun was about to set, Taelor left his companions, saying he wanted to visit Ukanzah by himself. But the truth was he wanted to be alone. It felt like a whole age since he had had some privacy. He wanted to take a walk in his solitude, in the fresh evening air.

He had been gone a quarter of an hour when he spotted the man. He was walking toward Taelor, but he wasn't looking where he was going. He was strolling along, cleaning underneath his fingernails with a small knife. And although he was still dressed all in black, a scarlet silk scarf was draped over his shoulders. He had dark olive-brown skin, a goatee, and a thick head of coal-black hair that spiraled in tight curls atop his head. Taelor slowed his pace, watching the man, and finally, feeling Taelor's gaze upon him, the man turned to face Taelor, two intensely dark eyes beneath bold eyebrows locking with Taelor's. A smirk played on the man's face.

"You," he said in recognition, chuckling slightly. "I liked what you did last night. That was good entertainment."

"The man deserved it," said Taelor awkwardly.

The dark man shrugged and with a gesture of agreement, said, "Most men do."

When Taelor gave no response, the man said, "I was watching you from across the room."

Taelor became uncomfortable. "Do…" he struggled, "…you know who I am?"

"No," said the man, "Should I?"

Taelor hesitated but said, "No."

The man chuckled warmly. "You're a terrible liar. But at least you're very beautiful. …I thought you were carved from some marble."

The comment made Taelor feel embarrassed. But the man only smirked again.

"Do you know who *I* am?" he asked of Taelor, his sharp eyes looking right into Taelor's over his hooked nose, his head tilted toward him.

"I don't," said Taelor.

"Have you ever heard the name Pascale before?" the man asked.

"No. I don't think so."

The man smiled. "I suppose that's good. And what would your name be?"

"Tev," Taelor answered.

"A very strange name," said Pascale. "I'm not sure it suits you."

Taelor looked to the ground before asking, "Are you from Espuilida?"

Pascale gave a small nod of his head, a glint in his eyes. "I suppose you haven't met many people from Espuilida? Most Espuilidans are so in love with their beautiful islands; they don't ever want to leave."

"I would like to visit one day," Taelor said politely.

The man smirked. "You would be well received there."

"I've had Espuilidan wine a few times. It really is the finest there is."

"Espuilidan wine, there's nothing like it," the man smiled, "I've brought a cask with me because I won't drink anything else. . . . With you, I would share it."

"I. . . Well, I should probably get back to my traveling companions."

"Making an excuse not to drink Espuilidan wine?" Pascale asked. "I'm offended. Anyway, walk with me back to the inn? You're still staying at The Tiger's Tail, yes?"

"Yes," said Taelor, and the two began to head there.

"So. . ." Pascale started after a moment's silence, ". . .it's strictly women for you, is it?"

"Uh, yes," Taelor said.

"Hm. . . If a soldier carries a sheath without a sword, there's no point, correct? And if he carries his sword without a sheath, that's dangerous and stupid, no? Do you enjoy the beauty of flowers but not trees, the moon but not the sun?"

"You shouldn't look at the sun," Taelor said uncomfortably.

"Ah, I see," said Pascale, "You abide by what people think you should and shouldn't do. . ."

"I try to," said Taelor. "I haven't been very good at it lately."

Pascale laughed. "I've never been good at it. But I've never tried to be. . . . That's what led to my woman kicking me out."

Taelor was taken aback by how open Pascale was. He didn't know what to say.

"I have two daughters," Pascale continued. "Very beautiful girls. But the woman doesn't want them to see me again. But of course, I do, in secret. And I do whatever I can for them with money. ...When you love people, it doesn't matter anymore *what* it is you do to help them. Would you agree?"

"To some extent," Taelor answered, perhaps more uncomfortably.

"Can I trust you will still want to be my friend after I tell you what I do?" Pascale asked.

Taelor gave no answer. He feared he knew, and Pascale saw it in his face.

"I never harm women or children," Pascale defended himself. "I refuse it. I also won't kill any man I find beautiful."

Taelor smiled darkly. "At least I'm safe," he said half-mockingly.

But Pascale laughed loudly and gladly.

"Why are you so quick to trust me, and why are you telling me all this?" Taelor asked.

"I can tell when a man is trustworthy," said Pascale, "and I'm an open book. I was also hoping that, in turn, you tell me about yourself. I'm quite curious to know. You are from Minear, and you're a noble, but you have a very strange name. You're on a quest of some sort. ...And I wonder how and why you lost a hand. There must be an interesting story behind it..."

Pascale made Taelor feel very uneasy. He wondered whether he could be some sort of spy. He even wondered if he could have been sent to kill him and was trying to confirm that he was, in fact, Taelor Pevrel.

"I make you uncomfortable," Pascale noted, stating it bluntly.

"You *do* make me uncomfortable," Taelor agreed.

To his surprise, Pascale laughed again. "I do tend to. I don't talk to people often. I'm not very good at it. Forgive me."

When they arrived at The Tiger's Tail, Taelor noticed a certain tenseness in the people he passed in the common room with Pascale by his side.

Lance, Leygon, and Rendy were sitting at a table in the far corner, away from the crowds. Taelor introduced them to Pascale and Pascale to them. Pascale looked them all over and said, "Two lord-knights and your squires?"

"Not quite," said Taelor. "I only met Rendy the other day," he said, gesturing to the boy.

Rendy gave something of a smile. It seemed that all three of them, Lance, Leygon, and Rendy, were unsure of how to receive Pascale. But Pascale took the seat next to Leygon and across from Lance, and Taelor sat next to Rendy.

"Who here drinks wine?" Pascale asked.

"I do," said Lance, "But as of now I've got a belly full of ale."

When Pascale looked toward Leygon and Rendy, they shook their heads.

"I have a cask of Espuilidan upstairs," said Pascale. "I already offered a cup to my new friend, Tev. He declined, but perhaps he's had a change of heart…"

"Are you a merchant?" asked Lance.

"No," said Pascale, "I used to be. But I was a merchant of olive oil, not wine. …I was also an actor for a time, but I got fed up with memorizing all the lines…"

"Why are you offering us your wine?" asked Lance.

"Because I'm a generous spirit," said Pascale with a gesture of open arms that expressed offense. A two-inch-long black beetle appeared from under the table and started crawling in Pascale's direction. Without tearing his glance away from Lance, Pascale crushed the beetle with his fist. Then, pulling a bright red handkerchief out from his pocket, he wiped off his hand.

Lance exchanged a look with Taelor.

"I don't have many friends," said Pascale.

"I wonder why," said Lance.

Pascale chuckled. "That is why I am offering you my wine."

Taelor was quite amused. "I'd like some," he found himself saying.

Lance and Leygon looked concerned. "Right," said Lance to Pascale, "Well, I'm coming upstairs with you and making sure you don't do anything... funny..."

"That's good. I like that," said Pascale, and he let Lance follow him up to his room.

When they came back down and joined the table, Pascale had a cup of wine in each hand and gave one to Taelor, then began to drink deeply from his own.

When Taelor put the cup to his lips, Leygon exclaimed, "Are you sure that's not... uh..."

"Poisoned?" Pascale finished for Leygon. Getting up and grabbing a vacant chair from a nearby table, Pascale sat back down and reclined his legs on it. "No, sweet boy. Poison is not my style. Here," he said, spreading his arm across the table, "give it to me, and I'll drink from it first."

133

"I wouldn't have let him poison it, would I?" asked Lance. But Taelor obeyed Pascale and gave the cup to his open hand. All eyes were on Pascale as he took a sip, and he waited a while before suddenly startling everyone within earshot by clapping his hands together piercingly loudly. "Look at that, still alive!"

Lance had been looking at Pascale with a hard expression, unamused and wary. Pascale handed Taelor back his cup, and Taelor took a swig. The taste alone made him feel as if he were under the hot sun of Espuilida, his heart filled with a sweet love. "Delicious," he said to Pascale.

"So are you," Pascale winked.

Lance shuffled. "You're a creep," he stated.

Pascale only smirked and again said, "So are you."

The Espuilidan wine was strong, and it sent Taelor into a deep slumber that night. Pascale had filled his cup a second time, and Taelor, being especially weary, retired himself early. He slipped into bed, pulled the covers to his chest, and folded his arms atop. Lance had made fun of how he slept, on his back, so straight and composed. He said he looked like he should be in a coffin rather than a bed. Taelor chuckled slightly, but that comment stirred an uneasiness inside him.

The voices of the witches whirled in his head again: *like thy father, thou wilt be slain by the hand of thy son.* But at this moment, he fell asleep before anything had the time to cross his mind. He dreamt of being back in his father's castle, now Alene's castle. In his dream, he felt happy and at peace to be back. Alene and Nadir were smiling at him.

And in under a week, he was back in reality.

Part 3

Chapter 9: The Return of the Prince

The journey back to the castle of Minear went smoothly. They rode in a wagon. Pascale had journeyed with them, but on the road, Ukanzah had left them. She had heard the singing of her people and left Taelor's company to join them. Taelor was saddened by this at first. Lance had said, "Did you expect to bring her back with you?" and Taelor didn't answer.

Then when Lance implied Taelor's attraction to her, Taelor simply said, "I cared for her well-being."

"But still, you wanted to bed her," Lance jested.

Taelor gave him a sharp look, but Pascale said, "I think she only liked women." There was an awkward silence at that.

On the journey, Taelor revealed his true identity to Pascale. Pascale was silent awhile but then stated, "You did not kill your father out of a thirst for power. He must have done something evil." Taelor, pleasantly surprised, nodded solemnly.

When they arrived, Pascale, rolling his cask of wine beside him, asked where the best brothel in the city was.

Taelor said, "I would not know."

And Pascale chuckled. "I was asking Lance."

Rendy looked in wonder at the castle. "Is that where I'll live?" he asked, wide-eyed.

"It is." Taelor smiled.

Leygon was just as pleased to be back as Taelor was.

Taelor was greeted by the same smiles of Alene and Nadir that he saw in his dream. Alene had embraced him with tears rolling down her cheeks. Then her expression fell when she noticed that Taelor had lost a hand. "What happened?" she asked horror-stricken.

"'Tis a long story," he replied. "I will tell thee some other time." Nadir had a cryptic look on his face.

"This is my new friend, Pascale," Taelor introduced, "Pascale, this is my half-sister, Alene." Pascale took Alene's hand and kissed it.

"Good looks run in the family, I see," he said. Alene smiled courteously.

"And this is my uncle, Nadir."

Pascale looked Nadir over and said, "Sometimes they skip a generation."

A wry grin appeared on Nadir's face. "I am charmed by thy new friend," he said to Taelor unconvincingly.

Young Rendy proved the more charming during his introduction, ignorant to the courtesies of the court though he was.

Taelor had appointed Lance as head of the Queensguard, the greatest honor a knight could hope for, and had given him gold in plenty. There were still those in Minear who shot Taelor dirty looks and called him names that degraded his honor, but Pascale had offered to kill all of those. Taelor refused the offer but told Pascale that he may yet call him to service. Pascale, twirling his dagger between his fingers, smirked and gave a small nod of his head.

Taelor made Rendy his and Alene's ward. He had his own chambers and was struggling to get used to being treated like a lordling. But nothing, Taelor thought with a chuckle, could make Rendy start acting like a lord.

Taelor had decided to join Alene and Nadir during their council meetings. Nadir was good with finances and resources, and well-practiced in diplomacy. He had grown to understand the Pevrel enemies through years of observing their moves and attitudes. He said to Taelor, "He who knows his enemies will always be a step ahead of them."

Nadir was a true Pevrel, Taelor had always thought. He was like the Pevrels of old. Shrewd, and the only one left who had a strain of foresight, Nadir sometimes had visions and premonitions. The late King Naelor had envied that; it added to his resentment of Nadir if it was not the cause of it. Taelor listened to Nadir closely during council meetings, and it was quite some time before he shared his own mind. Nadir admired him for that. There was no friction between Minear and other kingdoms, between Pevrel and other houses, at this time, but Nadir was always wary, especially of King Sederr in Laiden, just north of Minear.

Leygon's duties became fewer, but Taelor always spoke with him alone at evening. "I killed my father," he said to him one night, "and now the least I can do is become a man he's proud of. Everything I've done thus far has been an act of idiocy."

Leygon told him that to make Naelor proud, Taelor would have to be stern, hard, unforgiving, and prideful. He said that to make Naelor proud, he would have to be a strong, brave warrior and that he couldn't be now, with his swordhand gone.

"Become a man *you're* proud of," Leygon said.

Alene and Nadir had suggested getting a prosthetic hand crafted for Taelor to fit onto the stub at the end of his right arm. "What would be the point?" Taelor had asked, though in truth he appreciated the idea of having a fake hand where his lost limb was, just to have something there, regardless of whether it was able or not. They had measured his left hand, the palm and the length of his fingers and thumb, and gotten its counterpart made by Zoven, the finest craftsman in Minear. Zoven worked with the court physician, Bengir, who was a well-learned scholar of the human body, to make the prosthetic hand out of materials that would measure to around the same weight as Taelor's living hand. By Taelor's request, they painted the hand black and gave it a glossy finish. Taelor now had a black hand where his stub was. This earned him the name Blackhand, though most used it in mockery, remembering Naelor's demise.

Lance had been training Rendy in swordsmanship and archery; Rendy showed a true talent for the latter. Rendy joined Taelor and his men on hunting trips and seemed to enjoy nothing more. He was a good hunter and was well liked by all those who knew him. Alene would often dote on him and pick outfits for him. But Rendy hated wearing "fancy" clothes.

Meanwhile, there was a new face in court, a beautiful woman with long red hair and a willowy figure. She would look Taelor's way every now and then and shoot him a bright smile. One day, Taelor plucked up the courage to introduce himself to her.

"I do not believe we have yet become acquainted," he said, bowing before her as they crossed paths down a corridor.

"We have not," she answered, curtseying. "But I believe you know my sister."

"And who is your sister?"

"Your sister," the woman smiled. "The queen."

Taelor, taken aback, said, "Alene? She did not tell me she had a sister."

"Well, here I am," the woman chuckled, twirling her auburn locks. "My name is Jaylinn, by the way."

Taelor took her hand, kissed it, and said, "The pleasure is mine, Jaylinn." Then after some thought, he said, "We are not... uh…"

"Related?" Jaylinn laughed. "Oh no, we are not. I am Lady Elanna's legitimate child. My father was Lord Gregir."

Taelor smiled. "That is well."

Jaylinn laughed happily. "It is, isn't it?"

After a moment of awkwardness, Taelor said, "Lady Jaylinn, would you do me the honor of dining with me tonight?"

"Nothing would please me more," Jaylinn smiled brightly.

That evening, Jaylinn feasted with Taelor in his chambers, and they were each drinking a lot of wine.

"So, you are six-and-twenty," Taelor said, "and a maiden..."

Jaylinn mocked offense. "Are you calling me old?"

"No," Taelor said. "Not at all. 'Tis just, a woman as beautiful as you... one would have thought you would be a man's wife by now."

Jaylinn laughed. "I have had many suitors. But maybe, have you thought, Your Highness, that it is a woman's choice, also, whether or not she wants a romantic relationship?"

Taelor looked puzzled. "You have not been interested in romance?"

"I'm afraid not," said Jaylinn. "There are other things women are interested in, you know... Like my sister, I play the lute, I write poetry—granted, I'm not nearly as good as my sister at either, and I cannot sing as well as she—but I draw better, and I sew. ...I would say I've kept myself rather well-entertained without a man."

Taelor smirked. "You have never lain with a man before?"

Jaylinn smiled uncomfortably. "No," she said. "I would not, not before marriage."

Taelor, endeared, was very respectful of Jaylinn the rest of the night, and when they departed, he gave her nothing more than another kiss on the back of her hand.

The next morning, before the council meeting started, Taelor said to Alene, "You did not tell me about your sister."

Alene chuckled. "She catches the attention of men well enough on her own."

Taelor grinned. "She is very sweet," he said, "like thyself."

Alene suppressed laughter. "She *is* very sweet," she agreed.

"I quite like her," Taelor said.

"Well, thou would be pleased to know she feels the same. She speaks of thee all the time."

"Really?" Taelor smiled.

"Oh, yes," Alene exclaimed, "She has been *Prince Taelor*-ing my ears off."

"What has she been saying?" Taelor asked eagerly.

"Oh, that Prince Taelor is so handsome and tall, and he has such nice hair and such pretty eyes, and how sexy it is that he's missing a hand…"

"What? She thinks that's *sexy*?"

Alene nodded. "Women like strange things sometimes."

After a moment, Taelor asked, "What would thou think if I asked her hand in marriage?"

Alene, slightly taken aback, said, "You would have my blessing, indeed."

Taelor smiled and leaned over to kiss Alene on the cheek.

"How did you lose your hand, anyway?" Alene asked. "And how did it heal so quickly?"

"If you must know," said Taelor, "witches."

"Witches?" Alene exclaimed.

"Yes, witches… Now, where is our uncle?" Taelor said, looking over at the empty chair where Nadir usually sat.

Right at that moment the door opened, and Nadir swiftly walked through. "So sorry I'm late," he said, and he took his seat, and the council meeting began.

A few days later, Taelor summoned Jaylinn to his chambers. Taelor got a sapphire necklace made especially for Jaylinn; on the silver backing was engraved the words, "To Jaylinn. Love, Taelor." The sapphire was a flat oval and it hung from a silver chain. Taelor kissed it before presenting it to Jaylinn.

She took the necklace in her hands meekly and kissed the sapphire. "Thank you, Prince Taelor," she said sweetly.

Taelor smiled upon her. "I hope it makes you happy."

"It does," she said.

"Would it also make you happy, sweet Jaylinn, if I asked your hand in marriage?"

A smile lit up Jaylinn's face. "That would make me the happiest woman in all the world."

Taelor returned her smile, then asked if he could kiss her. She nodded her consent, and when their lips touched, Taelor felt as if the planets aligned.

They wed within the fortnight. Alene, Nadir, Leygon, and Lance were all of very high spirits during the wedding ceremony and feast. But Pascale had said to Taelor, "Are you aware of what kind of woman she is?"

"What do you mean by that?" Taelor questioned.

"It is not my place to say," Pascale answered.

"Pascale, I command you to speak."

"She," Pascale began, "is a redhead. …There are some who might say she is a witch…"

Taelor laughed. "That is ridiculous, Pascale. I have met witches. She is not one."

Pascale joined his laughter. "It was just a joke."

Taelor, gleeful, said, "I think I sense some jealousy, Pascale." Taelor laughed and shook his head, then returned to Jaylinn's side.

Taelor awoke the next morning feeling like he had the most amazing night ever. He turned over and saw Jaylinn sitting against a propped-up pillow next to him, naked.

"Good morning, handsome," she said, planting a kiss on his face.

"Good morning," he smiled.

Then, Jaylinn reached over her side of the bed and handed him a piece of paper.

Taelor, feeling groggy, took it from her and saw that it was a sketch of himself sleeping. It was excellent, both the likeness and the style.

"Wow," was all he could say.

"Do you like it?" Jaylinn beamed.

"I love it," Taelor said. "It is really good."

"So are you," Jaylinn smiled, kissing Taelor's face again.

Not long afterwards, Jaylinn began to show signs of pregnancy. Taelor was very excited but feared the possibility that the baby may inherit his loss of right hand.

At four months, Jaylinn's bump was large enough for one to assume her pregnancy was nearing its end. Bengir said she was with two children. "Twins," Jaylinn and Taelor gasped. "Yes, twins," confirmed Bengir.

Three months later, the court received word that King Raylir of Haseidin had died from natural causes. Taelor still remembered the face of Raylir, dark and strong and mirthful. Then Taelor wondered what his life would have been like now if Raylir's stepdaughter, the young Lady Ethellas, had lived and been his wife. He tried to picture her face but found that he couldn't. He remembered how beautiful she was, but her face was lost to him. It seemed strange that he remembered Raylir's so well. Perhaps the thought of Ethellas made him so upset that his memory decided it was better to neglect her.

Nadir seemed happy about Taelor and Jaylinn being married and about the babies they were expecting. But in his heart, he felt like Taelor and Alene would have been a better match. Centuries ago, it was common for Pevrels to marry each other during the height of their empire. They wanted to keep their bloodline pure to ensure that the Foresight would run strong in them. But when the empire fell after invasions from the east, the Pevrels began marrying for political alliance, to gain western allies and strengthen the west against the threat from the east. But that was long ago, and the east had since left them alone. Naelor thought that in marrying Taelor to a Lady from Haseidin, Pevrel would be the only House in the west with an eastern ally and that with such moves, the Pevrels would eventually have the power to dominate once more. But after the stepdaughter of the King of Haseidin was murdered on Minearan soil just hours before the union was to be, Naelor had promised his traumatized son some years of freedom. That was six years past, and Taelor had turned three-and-twenty that autumn season.

One morning, during council, there was an extra presence. Taelor, Queen Alene, Jaylinn, and Nadir were joined by Lord Eckert, narrowly known to be Nadir's lover. Nadir's face was pale and grave and his manner somewhat frantic. Motioning toward Eckert and barely looking at Alene and Taelor, he said, "You might be wondering why Lord Eckert is here today..." Taelor looked over at Eckert, at his pale face and paler hair, youthful, delicate features, and indifferent countenance. Listlessly, Eckert refilled his chalice with the jug of wine which had never been present during these morning councils previously. "He is here because he keeps me calm," Nadir finished. Eckert took a swig of wine, a bored expression in his light eyes and pouty lips, and uttered less than a greeting to his queen, Taelor, or Jaylinn.

"What is it?" Alene asked as Taelor helped Jaylinn take her seat and he sat beside her.

"The Haseidin army, the largest and greatest army of the east, is coming for Minear," Nadir spoke, his voice quivering. "A siege. My spies report that Queen Ethil is behind it. They are crossing the great waters as we speak."

After a moment of shock, Taelor said, "Then we must rally the west and meet them on open field."

"Tyniad will come to our aid in the blink of an eye," said Alene.

"As would Crole," said Taelor. "Their naval forces could ambush the Haseidis. They, of course, lack in number what it would take to defeat them. But they have been loyal allies of ours since my parents wed."

"But does their loyalty extend to going off on a suicide mission?" Nadir asked dryly. "And we will not meet them on open field. We have the advantage of the castle's stronghold. Only a fool would choose to abandon it."

"If we allow them to wreak havoc upon our queendom, haven't we already lost?" Taelor asked heatedly.

"No, Taelor, we have not," said Nadir with cold impatience. "Only if they break entry into the castle have we lost."

"Which is quite likely if we choose to remain! We will only be luring them in!"

"Taelor," Nadir spoke, exasperated. "I know of what I speak. And thy mind is not yet a man's."

"And what battles have you fought in, Uncle, let alone strategized?"

"None," Nadir admitted. "But I have spent my life listening and learning." After some silence, Nadir said, "We would be better off with Crole's army coming to us, along with Tyniad's."

"And what of Laiden's?" Taelor asked.

"Do you really believe Laiden would come?" asked Nadir. "Sederr would not send his men. He cares not for ancient vows, he hasn't a shred of honor, and would only be triumphant if ruin came to Minear. You know that."

Out of the corner of his eye, Taelor saw Eckert pouring himself yet another cup. Sunlight streamed through the great window and hit the wine inside the jug, making it appear like liquid rubies.

"Then," said Taelor, "we'll send word that Haseidin is coming to conquer all the west, that this is as much a threat to him as it is to us. He'll come then. ...And for all we know, Haseidin could be..."

"I would presume not," said Nadir. "Ethil is just a distraught mother coming for her long last revenge on Minear. She has been waiting for Raylir's death to carry it out."

"What makes you so certain she doesn't want more?" Taelor asked.

"I know the ways of a woman's heart."

Taelor cocked an eyebrow.

A cry came from Jaylinn as she held her stomach, bent over in pain.

"Are the babies coming?" Taelor gasped.

"No," said Jaylinn. "Just..." She broke off, wincing.

"Take her to Bengir," said Nadir, softened.

And so Taelor did.

The babies were not to come until Minear's fateful day...

Chapter 10: The Siege

Jaylinn's water had broken, and she lay on the bed in the room of Bengir. Inside the castle it was as if time had come to a halt, reality but a dream, everything but the tension in the air just a hazy vision, for outside, Haseidin's scores of thousands of men were approaching quickly. At this moment, they looked like just a swarm of ants from outside the window, but soon they would be surrounding the castle with all their steel and flying arrows.

"Please…" Jaylinn breathed, "Taelor, go not. Stay here with me…"

Taelor sighed a desperate sigh. "Thou knowest I cannot."

Jaylinn knew in her heart of hearts that it was not even worth asking, yet she found herself begging again. "Lance will command… The babies…"

"I must be there. Thou knowest I must," Taelor said.

Jaylinn gave in. "But promise thou wilt come back."

Taelor swallowed. "I will."

"And quickly," Jaylinn pleaded. Tears rolled down her cheek. Taelor wiped them with a gentle hand, and kissed her lips, then her brow, then he turned to leave without looking back, his feet leading him where his duty called.

~

The sky was drizzling with rain, and all Taelor heard as he stepped outside was the sucking of sludge under his boots as he made his way through the men and to the edge of the rampart to greet Lance.

"Hopefully the rain picks up," said Lance. "These desert swine aren't well acquainted with rain."

Taelor didn't answer. Lance looked over at him. "You should go inside," he said. "What can you expect to do with one hand?"

"Be present," said Taelor, "with my men."

Lance gave something of a scoff. "There's a difference between courage and mere stupidity..."

"I'm not here so that I don't look a coward, Lance. 'Tis about honor; a knight should know that."

"Very well," said Lance, not coldly.

Taelor heard the splashes of someone running through puddles from behind. As he turned, he saw the boyish face of Leygon coming toward him. He was armed with a crossbow.

"No," was all Taelor said, in an authoritative manner.

"I can choose to fight for the queendom and my home," said Leygon.

"Thou art no knight," said Taelor, "and I will not let thee."

"I never asked your permission," Leygon replied determinedly but with a grin.

"This is no joke, Leygon," Taelor said sternly.

Leygon pointed to his left. "Yet Rendy is allowed to fight?"

Taelor looked over and saw the boy, crossbow already at the ready, looking down at the Haseidin army as they came ever closer.

Taelor turned back to Leygon, at a loss for what to say, but still clearly against the prospect. Finally, he turned to a knight behind him and said, "Knock my servant out and bring him into a chamber and lock the door."

Leygon had but a second to attempt protest before he was hit over the head, his consciousness lost from him. The knight then threw him over his shoulder and carried him inside.

Lance tutted, shaking his head. "There was little honor in that," he taunted Taelor.

Taelor shrugged, annoyed.

"Well," started Lance, "I'm going down there. You, don't be a fool, and stay up here."

Taelor looked at Lance steadfastly. "Come back. When the battle is won, come back..." But the words were hollow as they left his mouth.

Lance nodded at Taelor, gripped his forearm, and went.

Taelor gazed at the oncoming Haseidin army. They must have been twice the number of the men of Minear, Tyniad, and Crole. In his heart, Taelor despaired, yet he tried his hardest to rid himself of it.

"Before we die," a gruff and familiar voice spoke from behind, "I want to know how you lost that hand."

Taelor turned to see Sir Gavin but did not respond.

Gavin leaned into him and said in a gravelly whisper, "Pleasuring yourself too hard, weren't you, and it just flung right off?" He laughed his hoarse and hideous laugh and drank heavily from his leather skin.

Taelor ignored the vulgar jest. "This is not the night I die," was all he said. But then he added, "My death has been foretold."

"With some luck," said Gavin, "it won't be the night I die, either. I'd be missed by the ladies too much."

Taelor couldn't help but smirk. "I wouldn't count on it."

Gavin laughed again, but Taelor did not join him. The Haseidin army was smashing down the great gate. Taelor turned and looked at the men about him. Most were putting on a brave face, but some were noticeably afraid.

"Tonight," Taelor began, in a battle voice he didn't know he had, "we will fight with a fierceness that Haseidin will regret having brought forth! Tonight, wives will be widowed, and children will be made fatherless. ...But as long as we fight with all the fury we've got, those children will not be orphaned. For we fight for our women! We fight for the children, the old, the weak, and for the honor and pride of Minear! We may fall, *but Minear will not!*"

The speech was met with fiery cheers.

"Now," Taelor concluded, "let us show Haseidin the great wrath it has awoken!"

Taelor's words were met again with great enthusiasm. The men of Haseidin successfully smashed through the gate and were now pouring in, their orange capes flying behind them, their banners getting wet in the rain. They began to form into a semi-circle around the castle front. Minear's battle horns sounded. Taelor thought he might have also heard drums in the distance, but then he realized it was the thumping of his heart. From far left to far right were the bright orange capes and banners of the enemy, the Polat hyena spiteful and mocking.

Arrows glided through the air as the din of clanging steel and battle cries rose to Taelor's ears from below. Taelor commanded the men from the rampart, their arrows soaring at his word. Taelor feared for Rendy, but the boy was skilled and smart, and his short stature worked in his favor. Sir Gavin took an arrow to the eye and fell at Taelor's feet. Taelor looked down at his body, more sorrow in his heart than he thought he would feel. But it was Lance he was concerned about. He tried to spot him in the chaos below, but he could not find his friend amid the mass of orange and blue.

The orange comprised a giant, and the noble blue was drowning in it. Taelor's stomach churned. The Haseidin army would butcher every last man fighting for Minear, cross the moat with their wooden planks (that Taelor had seen the enemy carry through), ransack the castle, and what they might do then, Taelor could not bear to think. He would rather suffer any torture imaginable at the hands of Haseidi than see his loved ones dead or assaulted.

Taelor knew, though refused to believe, that any hope he might have had was in vain, but now he saw it before his very eyes. There was no chance for Minear. His head swam about him. His queendom was sinking.

But then he noticed a black cloud swirl in the sky above him, floating toward the great black steel hawk. It began to engulf it, and suddenly, a great, thunderous clang rang out. The men on the rampart turned their heads around and backed away, shielding themselves as best they could. The noise continued, a sound like heaven being ripped apart by something evil. Then, a proud and mighty squawk was heard echoing through the air, and huge, shiny black wings soared through the sky above. The Hawk of Minear was alive! It swooped down upon Haseidin's army, flying right into the men with great speed, knocking them down by the score, coming for all of them. Those Haseidin men that the Hawk had not already felled went running from harm's way in every direction. Taelor watched in triumphant disbelief, tears of relief filling his eyes, a victorious song in his heart. Minear was saved! They would not be defeated this day. His loved ones were safe.

Chapter 11: After the Siege

Taelor turned around, entered back into the castle, his soul light and free. He ran straight for Jaylinn to tell her of their great victory, about how the Hawk of Minear had come to life and saved them all. He strode down hallway after hallway, a smile of relief across his face; he could hardly believe Minear was all right. When he came to the room of Bengir and opened the door, his smile disappeared to be replaced with confusion and horror. There was a bloody sheet over a body on the bed which Jaylinn had occupied. Wet nurses were seeing to two babies, each with a head of black hair, one a boy and one a girl, but Taelor paid little notice to them. He found his hand reaching to the blood-stained sheet, pulling it down to reveal the face. The face of his wife was ghostly pale, and her skin shimmered with a thin film of perspiration. Her green eyes had a far-off look, and strangely, her mouth was curved in a smile. Taelor put his hand to her face, unable to speak or feel or do anything but just hold his hand there.

"I am so sorry," Taelor heard Bengir speak beside him, his voice soft and sorrowful. "So very sorry."

Taelor could give no response, not even a nod of acknowledgment. He wanted to cry, or scream, or break something, but he knew he couldn't physically do any of those. It was as if his body had been turned to stone.

"Both your children are healthy," Bengir said. "They are perfect."

Taelor wanted to be glad of that yet found that he felt no gladness. Finally, he drew his hand back from Jaylinn's cold and clammy cheek, turned away, and headed out, slamming the door behind him. He stormed back to the rampart. The live men of Haseidin were near gone, all scattered from this place. Few Minearan men lingered still at the rampart. Many had gone back inside to their loved ones or had gone down to make sure no Haseidi men fled into the castle grounds. The night stirred with something of a magical wind. It was the wind of glory, coming from the Hawk, no doubt. But Taelor climbed up onto the wall, looked down at the immense drop below him, into the stone and mortar all those meters below, and made the jump.

But the wind caught him. He floated down to the ground gently. Then a cold and powerful voice penetrated the very wind, speaking, "My son, thou cannot escape thy destiny."

"Father!" Taelor yelled back, but he could say nothing further.

"Thou hast children now," the voice of Naelor came again, but softer and kinder, and into his ear rather than the air about him.

Taelor nodded, a tear falling from his eye and rolling down his cheek.

"Go to them," said Naelor. "Do not underestimate a father's love."

Taelor nodded again and searched the air for some sort of physical manifestation of his father, to look into his face, but could see nothing. Then he made his way back into the castle, entered the room of Bengir once more, and looked upon his children swaddled in the arms of wet nurses. The girl was wrapped in a light blue blanket, and the boy was wrapped in a dark blue blanket. Taelor made his way over to the plump nurse swaddling his newborn daughter and asked to hold her. When the nurse handed the baby into his arms, Taelor's heart felt lighter, filled with such a warm love that he was momentarily distracted from his loss of Jaylinn. He looked into the face of his son, too, in the arms of the taller nurse, and felt a great love for him as well, despite the prophecy, and also despite Jaylinn's death in birthing the twins. He was but a babe, a little, innocent babe with smooth cheeks and big eyes, now shut, lost in sweet slumber. Taelor decided he would think up names for them this night and have them officialized on the morrow.

The rest of the night was a blur, and the next day Taelor awoke alone in bed, remembering Jaylinn was dead. He let out a despairing moan, grabbed the pillow beside him, and held it tightly over his face. A force began tugging the pillow away from his grasp. Taelor looked to see Leygon.

"Let me go back to sleep, then," said Taelor in a hollow voice. "And may I not awake this time." He rolled over.

Leygon said, "You will be pleased to know that Lance was injured in battle, but he'll be all right."

Taelor didn't respond.

"You said you would name your son Alor and your daughter Talene," continued Leygon, "but that you also wanted to give them second names, in the old language of the Elves."

"Yes," grunted Taelor. "And I'm glad Lance lives."

"I'll go search the library for the book on the Elf language and bring it up to you," said Leygon.

Taelor gave no response, and he drifted back to sleep as he heard Leygon exit his chamber.

When Leygon re-entered, Taelor awoke again, though barely. He knew not how much later it was, whether it was a quarter of an hour, or two hours later. But he had decided that time meant nothing to him anymore, anyway. It meant *absolutely nothing*. With a great effort, he pushed himself up so that he sat in his bed, his back against his pillow. Leygon handed him a big, heavy book with a dark brown cover; it looked very old, but it was well-preserved. No doubt it had been very dusty, and Leygon had wiped the dust.

"Thank you, Leygon," Taelor said sincerely. He opened the book and started turning the leaves. Leygon had seated himself in the blue cushioned armchair in the corner of the room. Taelor was grateful for his presence; he always knew that Leygon could pick up on when he didn't want to be alone.

After some hours, Taelor was set on the second names he liked for each of his children: for his daughter, *Melda*, meaning "beloved, sweet, dear," and for his son, *Dhaerow*, meaning "face of shadow, traitor."

After he dressed, he went down to the keeper of records, old man Catan, to tell him of his given names for his twins. Catan was a scholar, and he himself was learned in the language of the Elves; he was not fluent, but he knew Elvish better than anyone else in Minear. Indeed, very few knew any words, and very few saw reason to learn any. But Catan was an old man with no family, and books and records were his only friends; he spent all his time with them, and taught himself as much as he possibly could, especially in the worlds of medicine and healing, so that he could help Bengir, the court physician.

Taelor told the name of his daughter first, "Talene Melda," and after Catan had copied it into the Pevrel family records in perfect script, he gave the name of his son: "Alor Dhaerow."

Catan's face dropped, and there was something of a haughty look in his eyes. Knowing that Taelor's son was born first, Catan spoke, in his old and gentle voice, though there was passion in it now, "You cannot blame a babe for his mother's death in birthing him and thus christen him with spite."

Taelor's expression grew dark. "'Tis not for that deed that I name him." And with that, he made a sudden turn and swept out of Catan's keep of books.

~

That evening, after Taelor had spoken with Nadir, he ordered a search party to find Queen Ethil and bring her to him. The next morning, they returned with her as their prisoner. Queen Ethil looked decades older than Taelor's memory of her. Surely it was her grief that had been so ungentle to her face. Taelor was sitting on the throne in Alene's place (Jaylinn's passing causing her to isolate herself) with Nadir standing to his right when Ethil was brought before him. Taelor rested his eyes on her face for some time. Her appearance struck a chord with him. He saw in her face what he felt in his heart. He knew how grief could waste a person away. It had only been two days since Jaylinn's passing, but already he felt aged.

"Queen Ethil," he spoke finally. "You laid siege upon Minear; an aggressive act of war."

She stared back at him, unwavering, with those now-empty eyes of hers in her deep sockets.

"What should I do with you now?" Taelor continued. "I could put you in the dungeons, or I could even have your head. But that would only cause more war, more bloodshed, more bodies of men who didn't deserve to die... Plus, what good would it do? It would serve no purpose, just as your act of war didn't. I know why you did it: to avenge your late daughter, Ethellas. And I can understand that. Her death was a needless tragedy, and I can't imagine how much it hurts. But did your siege bring her back? No.

"But it caused many of my men to die, and many of yours." Taelor paused and looked into Ethil's proud face. But he knew the pain that lurked beneath her cold exterior and empathized. Her black hair was pulled into a tight bun at the back of her head, which made her face look all the more severe. "What would you have done," Taelor spoke again, "if you had come out victorious? Did you mean to murder me? Was that your motive?"

Ethil was still looking at Taelor haughtily. But Taelor decided he could not tell whether she was too proud, or too afraid, to give an answer.

"It matters not," Taelor settled. "What matters now is only what I do with you... And what I'd like to do is ask your forgiveness for the untimely death of Ethellas. It was an accident, a mistake, and although nothing of my doing, I feel a great sense of responsibility for it. ...If I could give my life to bring her back, trust me, I would."

Ethil, struggling to hold back tears and retain her air of unapologetic strength, gave something of a nod.

"And I would also ask," Taelor began, "you to be my ally, as Haseidin was meant to be to Minear, in honor of your daughter's untimely demise. Let there be peace and prosperity between us."

Ethil again gave something of a nod.

Taelor stepped down from the throne, approached Queen Ethil, and held out his right arm, his stub (he had forgotten his black hand), for it would have been rude to present his left arm. A new expression came into her face as she returned Taelor's eye contact and grabbed his arm to shake it. Taelor gave a small smile.

"Now, before I let you go, I will present you with two-hundred gold coins. Please accept them as a token of my well-wishing. Fare you well, and I look forward to many years of peace between our two great countries."

Ethil nodded with more assurance this time. "You are a wise and merciful prince," she spoke.

"I thank you," Taelor said. "May your journey back home be kind, Queen Ethil."

They exchanged one last look between each other, and Ethil then turned to exit the throne room.

Taelor watched as the guards closed the great throne room doors after her, and he felt proud.

"That was well done," came Nadir's voice, and as Taelor looked over at his uncle, he saw an uncommon smile on his face.

~

A few weeks later, rumors had surfaced that Jaylinn had slept with quite a few men in court, before Taelor had took her as his wife, and that she had a reputation for being promiscuous in Tyniad. At first, Taelor could not believe them to be true, but then, it appeared to make sense. She was an experienced woman, not maiden-like at all in his bed chamber. Distraught, he went to his half-sister's chambers and asked her if she knew Jaylinn to be that way.

Alene sighed and placed her hands on Taelor's arms. "I'm afraid so. I'm so sorry, Taelor."

Taelor stepped back, tears streaming from his eyes. "How could you do this? How could you let me marry her?"

Alene, indignant, said, "Taelor, that is why I did not introduce you to her to begin with. Do you understand now?" Alene's hand reached out to his arm once again, but he hit it away.

"Do not think to touch me," he said. "Moreover, do not think to speak to me."

And he turned away from her and slammed the door in her face. Alene stared at the door for some time, then burst into tears, picked up her lute, and played the saddest tune she knew.

Taelor stormed to Nadir's chambers. When his uncle received him, Taelor shouted, "Alene knew! She knew what her sister was like, what she was…"

"I'm so very sorry," Nadir said gently.

"We must remove her from the throne, do you understand? We must get rid of her, banish her from Minear!"

"Taelor, is that not a bit extreme? And she is queen. How would we do that?"

"You are a clever man, Uncle," Taelor boomed. "Figure something out."

Then Taelor turned away from his uncle and swept out of the room.

A short week later, Alene was deposed. She was told to gather her belongings and leave Minear. She would return at the price of death.

She wept when she looked upon Taelor for the last time, but he only met her gaze with icy eyes.

"You are my half-brother and I love you dearly," she spoke.

"You do not know what love is," Taelor answered coldly.

She turned away slowly and sadly and Taelor watched as she walked away from him, from Minear, and from her title of queen.

Taelor became king in her place.

Part 4

Chapter 12: The Bastard of Naygur

A scrawny young man called Pete was sitting at the local tavern in Haybridge with the rancher, Jem. They had a table off to the side, and Rayley and his gaggle weren't too far from them, arm-wrestling and trying to out-drink each other, and whatever else they were doing. Rayley had shaggy black hair, a finely chiseled square jaw, a cleft chin, and he had been getting on Pete's nerves even more than usual as of late.

"So, he really thinks he's gonna be king?" he asked Jem, scoffing as he watched Rayley making a fool of himself.

"He does, and so do loads of others," Jem said good-naturedly.

"Yeah, he has just what it takes," Pete said sarcastically as he took a swig of ale.

Jem shrugged. "Well, he was always one of my favorite lads back when he worked on the ranch. He always put in a long, hard day."

"And a good cattle boy makes a good king?" Pete sniggered.

"Guess we'll have to see, won't we?" said Jem.

"So… he's just gonna strut into the castle and say, 'I'm king now?'"

Jem gave a small chuckle. "That's his plan."

Pete rolled his eyes and took another swig of ale. "And King Taelor will just say, 'Oh, I guess you're right, you *are* the king,' and give him his throne?"

"Well, Taelor isn't the most beloved king, is he?"

"So, you think everyone will just want Rayley to be king instead? …Why's everyone so into the idea of him becoming king, anyway?"

"Well, it would be exciting to have a good old boy from little old Haybridge become king, wouldn't it?"

"Yeah, so exciting."

"Oh, he's coming over," Jem said, and Pete looked up to see Rayley approaching them with his hands around the waists of two pretty blonde girls.

"Aren't you going to stand and bow before your king?" Rayley asked them.

"I'm not bowing for you, Rayley, so you can just shove off," said Pete.

But Rayley laughed, his dark eyes gleaming, and he extended his muscular arm to ruffle Pete's hair. "I was only joking, don't get yourself in a huff." Then he said to the girls, "I love Jem. He's an absolute gem." The girls laughed, and Jem chuckled and smiled at him.

"It was a pleasure having him work for me," Jem said to the girls.

"You'll have to show that off to everyone once I'm king," Rayley bragged. Then he said, "Well, it was nice mingling with you peasants," before he and the girls turned to leave.

Pete acted like he was about to throw up. Jem looked at him and shrugged. "You know," he started, "you have two parents who love you very much. Rayley never had that. He doesn't even remember his parents."

Pete was silent awhile; then, he gave a small nod. "I understand," he said, "All those times I pitied starving children around the world, I should have been pitying *Rayley* instead."

Jem looked into his eyes with a somber expression. "'Tis something to think about…"

"Oh, yes, poor, poor Rayley…"

~

Prince Nadir entered into King Taelor's chambers.

"What of the bastard, Uncle?" Taelor asked.

"Our men are heading to the border of Laiden to identify him and bring him hither and to keep his mob in check."

"I cannot wait to meet my arrogant, treasonous cousin."

"You will not have to wait long," Nadir assured.

"Uncle," Taelor said gently. "If he's as much like Naygur in face as they say, just know, you may visit my chambers any time at night for a drink and talk."

"Thank you, nephew," Nadir said with a grateful bow of his head. "But I'm sure I'll see nothing of my beloved brother in this rebel and traitor."

Taelor nodded. "Even so, Uncle, come for a drink and talk."

After Nadir left, Taelor sat in his armchair and sighed. He was now four-and-twenty and his twin children one. They were beautiful, happy babies, and Taelor's time visiting them in their nursery (which he had recently doubled the guard of) was one of the few things that could make him feel half-alive anymore.

And recently, his mind had been troubled with the news of a bastard son of Naygur, Rayley, who sought the throne and had succeeded in accumulating hundreds behind his cause. For the short years Naygur was king, he had a new decree put in place. He, who decided he would never marry, stated that his bastard born of a mother of noble blood would be his heir. And this bastard at hand in the northernmost part of Minear claimed he was the son of one of Naygur's favorite ladies in court; Lady Shaley Hollard, who died of childbirth complications.

A short week later, Rayley was in the castle of Minear's dungeons. He did indeed resemble the portrait of Naygur. Taelor noted so immediately. He was as arrogant as Taelor expected, too. His face was smug, and he held himself like a prince although he had lived his whole life as a commoner. And he kept calling Taelor "little cousin."

Taelor visited him in his cell a couple of days later. The stone dungeons were dark and cold, and the smell of urine hung onto the air. Rayley was unkempt and looked crazed in the eyes. Taelor stood in front of the bars and stared at him awhile. Even in his condition, Rayley's looks did not fail him, Taelor had to admit.

"I do not want the throne anymore," Rayley said.

"You do," Taelor chuckled darkly. "You'd just prefer not to have it than to face death."

"I am your cousin," Rayley pleaded desperately.

"I killed my own father with my own hand," Taelor said plainly, then he turned and headed for the exit. He could not bear to be in there for long.

"At least I die," Rayley spat, "with the confidence that my soul will be going to heaven. Yours, on the other hand, is certain to go in the opposite direction."

"I would not be so confident if I were you," Taelor said. "And for that comment, I'll be adding a blow."

"What?" Rayley asked dumbly.

"Your head will be separated from your body in two blows."

Taelor watched as the light left his cousin's eyes and he sank despairingly to the ground.

"You could just let me go, and you'd never have to see me again," Rayley sobbed.

Taelor approached the cell again. His cousin's handsome face was contorted with anguish.

"I get no pleasure from this," Taelor began.

Rayley scoffed.

"I do not," Taelor said firmly.

"What, then?" Rayley asked.

"I don't trust you," Taelor said, "and I place the safety of my children, uncle, and myself above your miserable life."

Rayley broke into something like a laugh. "Ah, but my life's been far from miserable, trust me on that."

"Then why did you go and ruin it?" Taelor asked bluntly.

Rayley looked lost like he suddenly realized just how stupid he had been.

"I'll tell you this," Taelor said, "You look upon the most miserable man you have ever met, and I am a king."

"What's it like?" Rayley asked.

"Being miserable?"

"No," said Rayley. "Being king."

"Very much unlike how you imagined it, I presume."

"But you can do anything you want, and you have servants doing everything for you. You drink the best wine, eat the best food, wear the best clothes. Everyone has to treat you with respect."

Taelor was expressionless. But then he said, "Except yourself?"

"I thought," Rayley said matter-of-factly, "by Naygur's decree, I was the rightful king…" Then he sighed and said, "I acted arrogantly and foolishly, and I am ashamed. What can I do to right this grievous wrong?" He paused before saying, "A life of servitude. That would be humiliating."

Taelor looked at him blankly. "Goodnight," he said, and he turned to leave again.

"Please!" Rayley yelled, shooting up from the ground and clenching his fists around the bars.

Taelor was about to exit the dungeons when Rayley spoke again.

"At least get them to refill my water jug."

Taelor turned and nodded. "Have they fed you yet?"

"No, but I have no appetite anyway."

"You should eat," Taelor said. "What food would you like?"

After a moment's thought, Rayley said, "Some mashed potatoes."

"That's all?" Taelor asked, "No meat or sweets?"

Rayley shook his head.

"I'll also send for some Espuilidan wine. You have to try it."

"Thanks," Rayley said appreciatively.

"Anything else you woud like?" Taelor asked.

After a pause, Rayley said, "Some girls?"

Taelor raised an eyebrow. "I'm sorry?"

"Some girls, just to talk to, one last time. Please."

"What do you mean by *girls*?" Taelor questioned.

"Any girls. Ladies, I don't know…"

"I can get my uncle to find some for you," Taelor said.

"*Our* uncle," Rayley said, "he's as much my uncle as he is yours. He is a nice man. And," Rayley continued, tears filling his eyes and rolling down his cheeks, "he told me he loved me." Rayley choked up. "That was so nice to hear."

Taelor closed his eyes and drew a deep breath. "Rayley," he spoke. "You will get all the things you requested soon."

"Thank you," Rayley answered through his sobs.

Taelor looked upon him for the last time, then exited the dungeons.

Rayley had his head chopped off two days later, but in only one blow.

~

Nadir and Taelor were across from each other on blue-cushioned armchairs, a small wooden table in between them. Taelor had poured Nadir a spirit; it was sitting atop the table.

"I didn't... expect to react like this," Nadir struggled to say. "He looked just like him." He took out his handkerchief and dabbed his eyes. He was present at Rayley's execution. "But you had to do it. ...I just feel like I've watched Naygur die twice."

Taelor got up from his seat and put his arms around his uncle's shoulders.

"Thanks," Nadir sniffled.

"Drink," Taelor said, picking up Nadir's chalice and handing it to him.

"I never told you," Nadir said, refusing the drink and trying his hardest to regain composure, "but Naygur called for me after he drank the poison. He called himself stupid and died in my arms."

Nadir pulled out another handkerchief, buried his face in it, and wept.

Taelor could only watch, unable to find any suitable words.

When Nadir dried his tears, he picked up the chalice and drained it.

Then Nadir looked at Taelor and said, "You and the twins mean everything to me."

Taelor nodded in agreement. "And Eckert?" he asked with a small grin.

"Yes, and Eckert," Nadir said. "Although he loves wine and his own reflection more than he'll ever love me." He laughed a little.

Taelor chuckled. Then he said, "I think I should re-marry."

"Yes?" Nadir said. "I think you should as well."

"Does Sederr not have an unmarried daughter?"

"Yes, her name is Miriem. She is said to be very pretty."

"Do you know how old she is?"

"Seventeen, eighteen, nineteen…"

"Young, but not too young."

"I think you would make her very happy." Nadir managed to smile.

"But I am not happy myself," Taelor said.

"Well, I think *she* would make *you* happy."

"If such a thing is possible," Taelor said. "I hope so." Then after a pause, he added, "Do you think we can trust the daughter of Sederr?"

"She is a young girl," Nadir stated.

"Yes, but you don't think Sederr would attempt to put her up to anything?"

"I knew what you meant," Nadir said. "But no, I think Sederr too clever a man to meddle through a young girl."

"You're probably right," Taelor said. "But what if the apple does not fall far from the tree? What if the daughter is like the father?"

"We'll meet her first, what think you? Invite her and Sederr to Minear."

Taelor nodded. "Tomorrow, you will write the invitation."

Nadir gave a small bow of his head. "But now I bid Your Grace a good night. Sleep well, nephew. Better days are ahead."

"Goodnight, Uncle," Taelor said, then he called on one of his servants to escort Nadir to his chambers.

Chapter 13: Miriem

It was raining when Sederr and his daughter Miriem arrived in Minear, and the green stag on their banners was drenched. Taelor watched them arrive from the window, the sudden nervousness that came over him surprising him. He poured himself some wine before going down to greet his neighboring king.

He was waiting in the corridor with Nadir standing to his right, across the castle's entrance, the throne room just behind, when Sederr made his way inside, his daughter beside him with her face veiled, a few of his guards at their backs.

"Welcome warmly, King Sederr," Taelor bowed his head before the bald man. "Princess Miriem." His eyes tried to penetrate the black veil over the girl's face as he extended his left arm, took hold of her soft, pale hand and kissed it. She giggled.

"Thank you, Your Highness," King Sederr spoke in a formal tone, then more casually, "Last time I saw you, you were not quite yet ten. The most cheerless child I have met to this day."

Taelor nodded.

"Prince Nadir," Sederr greeted. "Good to see you."

"And you, Your Grace."

"I imagine you wish to change into dry clothes," Taelor said, "and are in want of supper and wine."

"But my daughter cannot eat or drink with a veil over her face," Sederr said.

"No," Taelor blundered. "She cannot."

"Have food sent to her chambers," Sederr stated.

"Uh, yes," Taelor said. And he called upon Leygon from behind him and told him to escort Princess Miriem to her chambers. "Princess Miriem," Taelor said, reaching for her hand to press his lips against it again. He realized how short she was. "You will find everything you need waiting at your pleasure. And if you do not, do not hesitate to call Leygon."

She curtseyed before him, stumbling slightly, then followed Leygon to her chambers.

"She is a silly girl," Sederr said when his daughter was out of earshot. "Better than a clever girl."

"I look forward to dining with you once you have changed," Taelor said.

"Your Highness," Sederr bowed, and another of Taelor's servants led the king of Laiden to his chambers.

King Sederr was not a charming guest. Over supper, he implied that he came all this way to lose something so that Taelor could gain it. The fact this marriage created a stable alliance between Laiden and Minear was not enough for him. He demanded payment as if his daughter were a goat. Taelor knew he had to stand up to Sederr so that the king of Laiden would not think he had control over him and could further use him.

"You act as if your daughter is the only maiden of high birth that exists in this world," Taelor said.

"Nay," Sederr said, "but she is, however, the most beautiful."

"Strange that you should cover her face—"

Sederr splashed the wine remaining in his goblet at Taelor. "You insult me by implying that I am a liar and my daughter is not the most beautiful! You are as arrogant as your father."

"Your Highness, please," Nadir said, "that is not what my nephew meant."

"Keep that sinful mouth of yours shut," Sederr spat, "I know what has been inside it."

Nadir's face went pale and blank, but he quickly regained composure.

"You go too far," Taelor said. "I will not, now, marry your daughter."

"Taelor," Nadir cried.

Sederr grunted and tossed the goblet down on the table. It made a loud *clunk* and rolled onto the floor. The king of Laiden was red in the face.

The following morning, Taelor bid his guests farewell. Miriem no longer wore a veil, and Taelor saw that she was indeed very beautiful, white as ivory with rosy cheeks, red lips, big blue eyes, and soft brown hair. She looked upon him longingly. In that moment, Taelor hated everything.

"King Sederr," Taelor spoke, as father and daughter turned to leave. "I think Minear and Laiden would profit greatly from an alliance. Let us not be at odds. Whatever price you ask for, I will pay. Gladly."

Miriem broke into a bright smile; Sederr smirked.

And so Taelor ended up presenting Sederr with fifty-thousand gold coins.

Within the week, Taelor Pevrel and Miriem Swinton were wed.

"Tonight," Pascale came over and said to them during the wedding feast, "I will be jealous of you both."

"Pascale…" Taelor said in a scornful but humorous tone.

The dark man smirked and bowed before he turned to leave.

"Who was that?" Miriem asked as if she were startled. Her wedding gown was a pale blue, and her jewelry was silver.

"That was Pascale," Taelor smiled.

"Yes, I heard you say his name," she said innocently. "But he can say things like that to you?"

"Well," Taelor said, "Pascale says what he likes, but he *does* what I tell him to."

"Does not everyone?"

"Yes, but… Pascale does things not everyone does, you see."

Miriem's eyes followed Pascale.

"He will take some getting used to, I am sure," Taelor chuckled slightly. "Worry not; you will see much more of Leygon than Pascale. You like Leygon, don't you?"

"Like him?" Miriem asked.

"Yes," Taelor smiled. "You're allowed to like him. You are not, however, allowed to love him."

Miriem's face dropped. "Why would I love—"

"Because everyone loves Leygon. But he's mine," Taelor laughed.

After a moment, Miriem let out a nervous little chuckle.

"He is," Taelor said. "My Leygon." He took another sip of his wine. "Please forgive me," he said, looking at Miriem, "I am just in a very good mood. It has been a long time since I've been able to experience mirth. And 'tis all thanks to you."

Miriem smiled. "I hope," she said, "I will always make you happy."

Taelor looked into her soft blue eyes. "My sweet lady, all you need do is exist, and I am happy."

Later that night, in Taelor's chambers, he brushed Miriem's hair away from her face and caressed her cheek with his thumb.

"My wife," he said.

"My king," she answered.

He moved in toward her and felt her soft lips against his. She began to take off her gown, and Taelor helped her, then removed his own clothing. Falling onto the bed, they performed the deed expected of them as an audience listened at the door.

Taelor awoke in the middle of the night to find that his arm was around Miriem, her head snuggling into his chest. Taelor smiled and kissed her head, then drifted back to sleep dreamily. Finally, he had a good woman. A pure woman.

~

Miriem continued to make him happy, despite her never being with child. He was a new man, lighter and more cheerful. Lance, most of all, could not believe the change in him; it made him feel good to see Taelor smile and laugh and joke. And Miriem grew and blossomed by his side. Four joyful years passed, but on the fifth, Miriem coughed blood and died. Taelor sunk deeper than ever, his grief consuming him entirely. Nadir had all weaponry and otherwise dangerous objects removed from Taelor's chambers, for fear he might take his own life. Taelor confined himself to his chambers as often as he could, writing poems about misery and despair. Sometimes he would go on walks with Leygon, and every time he saw a flower, he would pick it and say, "That is my Miriem," as he let it fall out of his hand onto the cold ground.

Part 5

Chapter 14: The Ball for the Twins

King Taelor was spending some hours alone in the royal gallery. It was afternoon, and the sunlight coming from the small ceiling windows shone down upon his features, his gaunt cheeks accentuated in it. Eleven years had passed, and Taelor was forty. He had no lovers after Miriem. Her portrait was exquisite; it captured all her loveliness and sweetness. But Taelor never granted it his attention. He avoided it completely. How cruel it was for her to have been taken from him, for death to have snatched someone so wonderful so soon. Her passing left an emptiness in his soul that he never even attempted to fill even partially.

He missed Alene terribly, too, he had to admit. He stood before her portrait now. It looked nothing like her. It was painted after she was banished, the artist having painted her from memory. Not only did the portrait not resemble Alene in face, but it also exuded nothing of her warmth or charm. The worst part was that Taelor forgot what she really looked like, and what her presence felt like, more and more with each passing day. And he wondered whether the portrait corrupted and twisted his memory of her. Sometimes he would think back on moments he had spent with Alene and see a face similar to the cold, painted one before him now. He hated the damn thing, and he hated looking at it. But what he hated most was how cruel he was to Alene. He never even tried to get in touch with her after he banished her. He regretted how cold he was to his sweet half-sister, but now, of course, it was too late. The most he could do was hope she was well.

Right next to the portrait of Alene was the portrait of Jaylinn. Another terrible likeness, this one painted from memory after her death. Taelor could not bear to look at this one for long at all—his heart held no warmth for Jaylinn. She had disrespected him to the highest degree. She was the mother of his two children, such was true, but they were a pain in his backside most of the time, anyway.

It was sweltering hot that day, and the afternoon sun shining through the glass made Taelor sweat. Giving the dreadful portraits one last look, he shook his head and turned to exit the gallery, realizing he needed a change of clothes. It was the birthday of his son and daughter, and a ball was to be held that night for all of Minear's nobility, court, and domestics. This was tradition, and today the twins turned seventeen, which meant they came of age.

Throughout their childhood, Talene was the energetic, skillful, and sharp-minded child. She was a strong rider and a good archer. She was even better at combat with sword than her twin brother, but Alor was a sickly child. He was bedridden for a few years from the age of six, and Bengir had tried to heal him by every means he knew how. He finally declared that the illness would eventually kill Alor, that there was no way to prevent it. But Alor had miraculously recovered by the time he was nine. Still, he was much weaker than most boys his age. And unlike Talene, whose mind was always quick and at the ready, Alor's head was in the clouds. He only had love for two things: poetry and animals.

During his sickness, Alor read through hundreds of books of poetry and wrote many a poem communicating his pain. But he never shared them with his father, nor his sister, nor anyone else. He always found it easier to share his thoughts and feelings with animals. Taelor had gotten him a black cat to keep him company, and Alor loved that cat with all his heart. And he had such an affinity with animals, particularly horses, that Taelor had lovingly told him once, when he was ten or eleven, that he could tame even the wildest horse, given the chance. These remained the only words of praise that Alor could remember from his father, and he held onto them dearly.

The twins looked so alike. Both had long, wavy black hair, Talene's falling to the middle of her back, and Alor's just below his shoulders, and though Talene's eyes were a light gray-blue like her father's, Alor's were green like his mother's.

Deep blue and silver draping covered the ball room's walls that night, and the long tables were covered with an elegant silvery layer. A cupbearer came to fill Alor's glass as he was eating his plate of spinach and egg. Everyone else had pheasant, deer, or beef on their plates, but Alor refused to eat meat because of his love of animals; this was hard for Taelor to accept at first, because Alor was already so weak and fragile, and refusing to eat meat would surely only weaken him further. But there was nothing Taelor could do or say to get Alor to change his stance.

Leygon, Taelor's advisor, along with Nadir, was seated at one side of Alor. Talene was seated at her father's right, and Alor his left. Talene was wearing a beautiful lilac gown that fell in subtle and airy waves to her ankles; it was a light, almost net-like material, and in it, she resembled a fairy. Next to her sat Rendy, their father's ward, the broad, strong, and energetic reddish-haired man who Alor was told had saved his father's life when he was a boy.

Rendy never paid much attention to Alor, but far too much to Talene. Alor always noticed Rendy's eyes drifting over to her, and sometimes caught the occasional grin, and even wink, in her direction. But he was one-and-thirty and would have been a commoner if his father had not taken him in; he was an orphan boy with no name or home, and Talene would be Minear's queen one day. She had the temperament and mind for it, and Taelor raised her with preparation for the position. For much of his life, Alor indeed felt like the throw-away child; he felt that it would have made little difference to Taelor or the kingdom if his illness had killed him. But he had since learned to disregard those thoughts and to simply live the best way he knew how.

The minstrel's song came to a close, and he began to play something that was strangely chirpy and melancholy at the same time. It made Alor feel uneasy.

Gray-haired Sir Lance came forth, a parcel in each of his hands. They were both wrapped in Pevrel blue.

"This one," he said, raising the parcel in his left hand, "is for our young prince." He smiled as he passed it to Alor.

"And this one," he said, raising the parcel in his right hand, "is for the world's prettiest little princess."

But instead of passing it to Talene, he laid it before Taelor.

Looking over at his father, Alor saw that he was grinning.

"Very funny, Lance," Taelor said.

"I thought so, too," Lance laughed, sliding the parcel over so that it was before Talene, giving her his silly wink.

Talene was laughing as well. Even Nadir looked amused, sitting next to Rendy with Lord Eckert on his other side.

After the meal, the dancing began. A violinist played a vibrant tune, the melody filling the whole room with joyous warmth. Alor remained at the table, and Leygon sat next to him with his wife, a small, plump, mousy-haired woman with deep eyes and a kind smile. Their six-year-old daughter, Poppy, was present as well. Alor knew how to make her laugh.

Talene was dancing with Rendy, and Alor felt his father's intent gaze on the pair. He always felt his father's gaze, but even more so when a sight displeased him... Alor would not dare look into his father's face at this moment.

When the festivities ended, Alor overheard Talene say to Rendy that she would talk to her father that night. And consumed with curiosity, Alor followed her, sneakily and light-footed, to Taelor's chambers. He hid behind a corner in the corridor when she knocked at the door and listened intently at the door after Taelor received her. The guards were not permitted to question or scorn Alor and acted as if they were unaware of his presence.

Alor could sense his father's energy even through the closed door; Taelor knew just what his daughter was going to say. Alor felt that.

"Rendy and I…" his twin sister began, her voice nervous but strong, "…would marry, with your permission."

Taelor did not speak for a while, his glance undoubtedly looking right into Talene, his face hard and cold.

"We…" Talene spoke again, "…are in love."

After another incredibly long pause, Taelor's voice came saying, "Thou art arranged to marry Prince Theodore, fifth son of Sederr of Laiden."

"I know," Talene sighed, "but I do not know him, so how do I know I could love him? And Rendy and I—"

"Talene," Taelor said. "Rendy is a commoner and twice thy age."

"He's the *king's ward*," Talene cried passionately, "not a commoner. And so what if he is twice my age?"

"It is unconventional," Taelor stated. "And if he were not my ward, he would be a commoner."

When Talene argued further, Taelor said, "Enough! Talene, thou wilt be queen of Minear. I want thy claim to be as strong as possible. *Minear needs* thy claim to be as strong as possible. …I have no doubt that thou wilt win the respect of the court and people with thy heart and judgment alone, but thou need to marry as well as a ruling queen can, for thy sake and thy children's."

Alor heard no response from Talene and could only guess that she nodded and that Taelor dried her tears and took her into his arms. And when he heard the handle at the door, he slipped away like a frightened rabbit and was unnoticed by Talene as she walked back down the corridor disheartened.

~

Taelor sat in his armchair, his head rested in his hand, looking downward. Talene and Rendy might yet run away together, he thought. Though he did not care. Let them. They would not get far before he sent Pascale after them.

Talene was strong-willed and rebellious at heart. This showed from a very young age. At times such as this, when the hardships of parenting presented themselves to him, he missed Alene and Miriem more than ever. If only they were with him, helping him, guiding him.

He felt compelled to visit Alene's portrait again.

He made his way to the royal gallery. The castle was quiet and still, it being late at night. He often wandered the castle in the middle of the night and the wee hours when he could not sleep, which was often. He liked the stillness and darkness, hearing only the sound of his footsteps and seeing the flickering shadows that the light from the torches produced on the stone walls and floor.

He took a torch off the wall by the gallery and entered in with it. He made his way to Alene's portrait. It was even worse when illuminated by the light from the flames. Part of Taelor wanted to set the thing on fire, be rid of it… But no. It was all he had of her…

"I'm sorry, Alene," he spoke to the portrait.

The oil likeness seemed to acknowledge his apology with a blink of her painted eyes. But then, startled, Taelor noticed that the portrait was morphing! He took a step back. Now before Taelor was none other than the face of one of the witches he had met some eighteen years ago in the forest. It smirked at him grossly. Taelor flinched.

"The time of the prophecy is nigh," it spoke.

Then, echoing around the gallery, was the ghastly cackling of all four witches. Taelor looked about him hurriedly, but could not see them, yet the sound of their horrid laughter swam around the room.

He was lying on the cold marble, coming to, when Leygon shook him awake with a concerned look on his face. It was morning. Taelor sat up, confused and horror-stricken. His back ached terribly.

"Are you all right?" Leygon asked.

"Yes, Leygon," Taelor said gently. "I'm fine. Just one of those nights…"

"This," Leygon said, in something of a stern tone as he picked up the cold torch from beside Taelor, "is dangerous. What happened here?"

"Wind blew out the flame," Taelor stated. But there were no windows that could be opened in the royal gallery.

Leygon looked Taelor in the face, knowing he was hiding something from him, though he could not tell what.

Taelor got to his feet, cracked his back while wincing, and with a smile, said, "Poppy is getting big, isn't she?"

Leygon tried to return the smile as he said, "Yes," but he was worried about Taelor and concerned about what he was concealing, though he knew better than to pry.

"You know," Leygon said finally, "I'm always here for you, like I always have been."

"Yes, I know that," Taelor said, smiling again. "Worry not about me, Leygon."

Leygon nodded reluctantly. "And there's something else…"

"What?" Taelor asked.

"In the night, Talene and Rendy ran off. Neither is anywhere to be found."

Taelor's features became very serious. "Nothing less than I expected," he said bitterly. "Bring me Pascale."

Now, Taelor had a reputation for being quite cold-blooded in his kingship, especially with matters involving Pascale. It was known that Pascale would creep around the castle, hiding in the shadows, listening for any bad or suspicious word spoken about Taelor. And deeming all such people as threats, Taelor ordered Pascale to kill them, in his own manner, sneakily and dirtily. Members of the court would sometimes wind up missing, and all became quiet because they knew why. Pascale was the most feared man in Minear, and Taelor was a much-feared—though a strong and respected—king. Minear thrived, and even King Sederr of Laiden knew to watch his steps.

"Taelor," Leygon said nervously, "don't do anything you'd regret…"

"I will not," Taelor reassured him. "I simply want Pascale to find them and bring them to me, and I will give each a stern lecture."

Leygon gazed at him in a way that said, *it better be only that.*

"Talene is my daughter and my heir," Taelor said sharply, "and Rendy has been like a son to me. Now, be on thy way; retrieve me Pascale."

"I know you would not harm Talene," Leygon stressed, "but Rendy... I've seen the way you have been looking at him. Talene loves him, remember. For whatever that's worth..."

Taelor gave no response.

Leygon started to turn to find Pascale as his king ordered, but halted, and said, "I admired you so much in our youth. You were so brave. And you knew what was right and what was wrong. But now... now, you really are your father's son."

Taelor went silent awhile, but then said, simply, "Find Pascale and bring him to me." So Leygon went on his way.

Taelor waited in the gallery, thinking of the witches, and of his ungrateful, treacherous ward, and of the audacity of Leygon.

Some fifteen minutes later, Pascale made an entrance, slipping in silently, his heavy gaze upon Taelor.

Taelor locked eyes with Pascale. "Rendy ran away with Talene in the night. Seek them. If Rendy puts up a fight, which he will, kill him. Bring Talene to me."

Pascale smirked. "Gladly," he said, with a small bow of his head, then he slipped out the door.

Chapter 15: The Foretold Doom

Alor was sitting in the armchair in his chamber, his black cat, Mori, on his lap. Alor was stroking him as he purred contentedly. This helped to ease Alor's anger. He was furious at Rendy for kidnapping his twin sister. That's what it felt like to Alor: *kidnapping*. It had been a whole day and night now. Alor heard rumors that his father had sent Pascale off to retrieve them, and he knew Rendy had it coming. He didn't know what, but he was glad of it; in fact, he would have liked to deal with Rendy himself.

The twins had never been close, so much was true, and oftentimes Alor felt like Talene was cold and indifferent toward him. But Alor forgave this because as much as Talene liked to believe the two of them were nothing alike, Alor knew they were connected. This was proven when at ten years of age, Alor randomly experienced an intense shooting pain up his arm. An hour later, he learned that

Talene had fallen from her horse and broken her arm. It was her left arm, the same one that Alor felt the pain in. From then on, Alor realized he could also feel her emotions when they were intense. Talene was a part of him, just as he was a part of her, even if she felt that way about Rendy instead.

One time, Alor remembered, Talene joined their father and Rendy and a few other men on a hunting trip, a crossbow in her hand, ready to shoot innocent animals with. Alor was already discontented, but to make matters worse, as Alor saw them off—after unsuccessfully trying to talk his sister out of hunting—he saw Rendy help her up onto her horse, and when Taelor wasn't looking, he took her hand and kissed it. Then, knowing Alor was watching, Rendy turned and gave him a smug look.

Visions of various instances of Rendy winking and grinning at his sister played over and over again in his mind.

He couldn't sleep all night, and eventually, he decided he wouldn't try any longer. Now, looking out the window, he saw that the sky was a deep blue, marking the coming of dawn.

"Rendy is a dead man," he said aloud to Mori, a smile curving his lips as he spoke the words.

~

When he breakfasted with his father, Taelor didn't speak a word, and Alor did not like the feel of his presence. Alor had little appetite and played with the egg and fruit on his plate more than eating it. His father hardly seemed to notice, and when Taelor finished his meal, Alor was free to leave. He went outside to the stables. The air was hot and sticky. It was an especially hot summer. Everyone around the castle was complaining about it. Their clothes stuck to their skin. Even the horses seemed a bit irritable. Alor spent time with each one of them, leaving each in a better mood than the one he found them in.

A horse had its head around Alor's shoulder as Alor was stroking its neck, when, suddenly, Alor felt a horror-filled scream of a young girl reverberate through his body. It was Talene's scream, no doubt about that. Alor stiffened, his eyes widening in sudden panic. Then but a moment later, he felt a stabbing pain in his chest, like a knife through the heart. Talene was murdered! Alor ripped away from the horse. Talene was murdered! Pascale was obviously her killer. And Pascale carries out the orders of his father. Alor threw himself on the ground, punching the grass, hot tears filling his eyes. He was horrified that his father would do this.

Getting himself up, he ran back inside the castle, down the hallway, weaving through all the people, pushing the ones in his path. He climbed the flights of stairs quicker than he had ever done before and made his way to his father's chamber. He was getting slower, but his adrenaline kept him moving. He heeded not his exertion.

Arriving at the door of his father's chambers, he ordered the guards to let him in. But instead, they notified Taelor that his son was come to visit him. With Taelor's permission, the guards let Alor in. There his father was, sitting on the windowsill by the foot of his bed, gazing out the window, his back to Alor. He didn't even turn around when he said, "To what do I owe the visit, Alor?"

"To what do I owe the visit?" Alor sneered. And with the heat upon him, he ran at full force at his father and pushed him out the window with a strength that only his passion could have given his body.

And both father and son—king and prince—fell through the shattered glass, falling *down, down, down...* until *thud.* King Taelor and Prince Alor were no more.

~

Nadir was in such a profound state of shock that he could hardly process the deaths of his nephew and great-nephew. He was haunted by the vision his mind had fabricated of both their bodies sprawled on the ground, their limbs twisted and grotesque, and his only consolation was that he had not seen this sight in reality. How awful it was. Yes, he had vestiges of the gift of foresight that House Pevrel possessed long ago. But he never foresaw this, could never even imagine this. It was just terrible.

In the late afternoon, word spread through the castle that Pascale was spotted arriving with Talene. *Talene*, Nadir realized. She was now the only other Pevrel left. His heart suddenly felt empty and aching. The deaths of Taelor and Alor were real to him now... brutally real.

Nadir made his way to the castle's entrance in a haze, waiting for Talene. The stone and marble of the castle seemed cold and lifeless now, despite the summer heat. The shimmering water in the moat, the bright grass, and the birds in the sky seemed like they were not really there. Nothing was really there. Not even Nadir. Or at least that was how it felt to him.

He had no idea how long he had been waiting there before he caught sight of Pascale on his black horse, Talene seated in front of him. She was still in her pretty lilac dress that she had worn to her birthday ball. As they came closer, Nadir noticed how distraught Talene looked. She was weeping hysterically. Obviously, word had traveled about the tragedy of her father and brother. At least Nadir would not have to be the one to break the news to her… He could hardly think straight, let alone be the bearer of such heinous news.

When Pascale crossed the moat on his horse and noticed Nadir standing there, he nodded a greeting to him and stopped his horse, getting down from it and then helping Talene down. She punched and kicked and kneed him the best she could, but Pascale was indifferent. And to Nadir's unfortunate surprise, when Pascale set her down, the first thing she did was turn to Nadir and scream, "Where is Father?"

Nadir felt the hollowness in his chest once again, even worse this time.

"Talene," he mustered. "We need to talk…"

"Where is he, now? Rendy didn't do anything wrong! I loved him, and he knew how much I loved him, but he didn't care! I felt my heart shatter into a thousand pieces!"

Her distress then overcame her. Nadir put his arm around her but could not think of what to say.

Pascale sensed something was wrong. "What happened?" he asked Nadir, and there was a concern to his voice most uncommon to his character.

"The king," Nadir began, not knowing how he could possibly try softening the blow, "is deceased."

Pascale's face, usually straight and unreadable, dropped.

Talene was frozen. Her glassy eyes, red and puffy from crying, looked up at Nadir.

"I'm afraid it is so, and I hate to be the bearer of this evil news. I can hardly believe it myself."

"How?" Pascale asked.

"Alor seemed to have pushed him from the window of his chamber," Nadir spoke. "Alor is dead, too."

"What…" Talene said feebly and pitifully, and she began crying even harder.

Nadir put his other arm around her as well, taking his great-niece in an embrace. And so they stood, Nadir and Talene with their arms around each other, and Pascale looking upon them. Then, a gust of cool wind swept over them, and as they released each other, Nadir saw a strange, unnatural cloud. It was black as smoke and resembled a hand perfectly, with four fingers and a thumb. He knew it was Taelor's black hand. And beyond it, storm clouds were rolling ever closer…

The End

Made in the USA
Middletown, DE
12 September 2020

18298539R00120